Gentlemen Prefer Blondes
&
...But Gentlemen Marry Brunettes

Gentlemen Prefer Blondes

&

...But Gentlemen Marry Brunettes

Two novels by Anita Loos

Vintage Books
A Division of Random House · New York

First Vintage Books Edition, March 1983

GENTLEMEN PREFER BLONDES
Copyright © 1925 by International Magazine Co., Inc.
(Harper's Bazaar)
© 1925 by Anita Loos
© 1953 by R. Anita Loos Emerson
© 1963 by Anita Loos
Originally published in 1925 by Liveright Publishing
Corp., New York.
... BUT GENTLEMEN MARRY BRUNETTES
Copyright © 1927, 1928 by Anita Loos Emerson
Copyright renewed 1954, 1955 by Anita Loos Emerson
Originally published in 1927 by Liveright Publishing
Corp., New York.

All rights reserved under International and Pan-American
Copyright Conventions. Published in the United States by
Random House, Inc., New York, and simultaneously in Canada
by Random House of Canada Limited, Toronto.

Library of Congress Cataloging in Publication Data
Loos, Anita, 1894-
Gentlemen prefer blondes.
I. Loos, Anita, 1894-
But gentlemen marry brunettes. 1983.
II. Title.
III. Title: But gentlemen marry brunettes.
PS3523.O557G4 1983   813'.52   82-48893
ISBN 0-394-71462-8

Manufactured in the United States of America

Gentlemen Prefer Blondes

The Illuminating Diary of a Professional Lady

TO JOHN EMERSON

CONTENTS

The Biography of a Book 9

1 Gentlemen Prefer Blondes 17
2 Fate Keeps on Happening 41
3 London Is Really Nothing 55
4 Paris Is Devine 75
5 The Central of Europe 99
6 Brains Are Really Everything 131

The Biography of a Book

There was a time a number of years ago when I found myself on a train, the de luxe *Santa Fé Chief*, travelling from New York to Los Angeles. We were a party of co-workers in the movies, en route back to our studio after a cherished holiday in New York, for we belonged to the elite of the cinema which has never been fond of Hollywood. There were Douglas Fairbanks, Sr, then at the beginning of his career in films but already a nation's idol, my husband, John Emerson, who directed the scenarios I wrote for Doug and a number of others, such as our publicity man, an assistant director, Doug's valet and Doug's trainer. In those carefree days of the silent movies, we traveled in large and exuberant groups.

Also among us was a blonde who was being imported to Hollywood to be Doug's leading lady in his forthcoming picture. Now this girl, although she towered above me (I weighed about ninety pounds) and was of rather a hearty type, was being waited on, catered to and cajoled by the entire male assemblage. If she happened to drop the novel she was reading, several men jumped to retrieve it; whereas I was allowed to lug heavy suitcases from their racks while men sat about and failed to note my efforts.

Obviously there was some radical difference between that girl and me. But what was it? We were both in the pristine years of early youth; we were of about the same degree of comeliness; as to our mental acumen, there was nothing to discuss: I was the smarter. Then why did that girl so far outdistance me in feminine allure? Could her strength possibly be rooted (like that of Samson) in her hair? She was a natural blonde and I was a brunette.

In view of the reception which was to greet *Gentlemen Prefer Blondes* a couple of years later, it appears I had stumbled onto an important scientific fact which had never before been pinpointed.

The light that dawned on me with that first revelation, began to illuminate an entire phase of my youthful experiences. I proceeded to go over the various blondes I knew. They were a very special group, for my lot had fallen in with the beauties of the films and the girls of the Ziegfeld Follies from which movie starlets were constantly recruited. And, in going over the list, I presently singled out the dumbest blonde of all, a girl who had bewitched one of the keenest minds of our era – H. L. Mencken.

Menck was my idol and a good friend too. He often took me to Luchow's for dinner; I was even included among his inner circle of beer lovers when they trekked over to Jersey City in those Prohibition days to drink a brew that was uncontaminated by ether. Menck liked me very much indeed; but in the matter of sentiment, he preferred a witless blonde.

The situation was palpably unjust. I thought it over as our train raced across the plains of the Mid-west, until finally I was prompted to reach for one of the large yellow pads on which I composed Doug's scenarios, and I began to write down my thoughts; not bitterly, as I might have done had I been a real novelist, but with an amusement which was, on the whole, rather childish. I have always considered grown-ups to be figures of fun, as children generally do, and have never been deceived by their hypocrisies. In those days I had a friend, Rayne Adams, who used to say that my slant on life was that of a child of ten, chortling with excitement over a disaster.

In fact, if one examines the plot of *Gentlemen Prefer*

Blondes, it is almost as gloomy as a novel by Dostoievski. When the book reached Russia, this was recognized, and it was embraced by Soviet authorities as evidence of the exploitation of helpless female blondes by predatory magnates of the Capitalistic System. The Russians, with their native love of grief, stripped *Gentlemen Prefer Blondes* of all its fun and the plot which they uncovered was dire. It concerns early rape of its idiot heroine, an attempt by her to commit murder (only unsuccessful because she is clumsy with a gun), the heroine's being cast adrift in the gangster-infested New York of Prohibition days, her relentless pursuit by predatory males (the foremost of whom constantly tries to pay her off at bargain rates), her renunciation of the only man who ever stirred her inner soul of a woman, her nauseous connection with a male who is repulsive to her physically, mentally and emotionally and her final engulfment in the grim monotony of suburban Philadelphia.

Given the above material, any real novelist such as Sherwood Anderson, Dreiser, Faulkner or Hemingway probably would have curdled his readers' blood with massive indignation. Scott Fitzgerald would have made, and indeed he did make, his readers shed bitter-sweet tears over such sad eventualities. But I, with my infantile cruelty, have never been able to view even the most impressive human behavior as anything but foolish. When, for instance, Albert Einstein evolved his world-shaking Theory and then admonished fellow scientists not to use it for the elimination of the species, it seemed to me the same joke as when a certain character in *Little Women* told a group of children not to stuff beans up their noses; with the consequence they could not wait to find some beans and stuff them up their noses.

As I began to put Lorelei's story down on my yellow pad, it became a mixture of fact and fiction. My heroine's real name was Mabel Minnow. Her birthplace, however, was invented and H. L. Mencken himself had a hand in the procedure. For I wanted Lorelei to be a symbol of the lowest possible mentality of our nation, and Menck had written an essay on American culture in which he branded the State of Arkansas as 'the Sahara of the Beaux Arts' (which he spelled *Bozarts*).

13

Therefore, I chose Little Rock for my heroine's early years; Little Rock which even today lives up to Mencken's choice as the nadir in shortsighted human stupidity.

I finished the few pages of what I considered to be merely a short sketch as our train was nearing Pasadena; it was time to pack up and get back to the frantic chores of the studio. I stuck the manuscript into the flap of a suitcase and forgot all about it for six months or more.

I might never have thought of Lorelei again, for I was a movie writer and wouldn't have dreamed that my heroine had any place on celluloid. But back in New York one day, I ran across the rumpled and smudged pages of my little critique and, in order to give Menck a laugh at his own expense (this being several blondes later than the one who had first inspired me), I mailed it to him.

Menck enjoyed my sketch, saw the point of it and, although it hit close to home and was an intrusion on his sentimental life, he suggested that the manuscript be published.

The story of its publication can best be told by quoting from the biography of Carmel Snow.

'When *Gentlemen Prefer Blondes* burst on a delighted world,' wrote Carmel, 'I took Anita Loos under my wing. She was literally under the wing of her tall, thin husband, John Emerson (she reached barely to his chest) and she claims that she held onto his coat tails when I took her around to parties, but our click was immediate and it extended even to our clothes. We were both dressed by Chanel, later by Mainbocher and most recently by Balenciaga.

'When I met her, Lorelei Lee was appearing serially in the magazine that was to become the impersonal love of my life. How we waited for each new installment in *Harper's Bazaar*! We didn't realize how nearly there were no further installments to follow the first one. Anita wrote *Gentlemen Prefer Blondes* as a short story and sent it to H. L. Mencken, that other great editor of the twenties. He had just left *Smart Set*, where he would gladly have published it, but he didn't think it was right for *The American Mercury* which he now edited. "Little girl," he now warned Anita, "you're making fun of sex and that's never been done before in the USA. I suggest you send it to Harper's Bazaar, where it'll be lost among the ads and won't offend anybody."

'Henry Sell was the editor in charge and fortunately saw the story first. "Why do you stop?" he asked Anita. "You've started this girl on a trip, go on." So, as Lorelei appeared one month in Harper's Bazaar, Anita was frantically writing the next month's installment. By the third month, ads for men's apparel, cars, and sporting goods began pouring into the magazine. This was the first time men had ever read the Bazaar – the newsstand sales doubled, then tripled. James Joyce, who had begun to lose his eyesight, saved his reading for Lorelei Lee. And George Santayana, when asked what was the best book of philosophy written by an American, answered, Gentlemen Prefer Blondes." '

After Lorelei's story ended in Harper's Bazaar, a friend of mine, Tom Smith, who was on the staff of the Liveright Publishing Company, asked if I would like to have a few copies of my story in book form to give friends as Christmas presents. I thought it an excellent idea and Tom thereupon had his firm print a sort of 'vanity' edition of a mere fifteen hundred copies (which accounts for the fact that those first few copies became collectors' items).

The first edition was sold out on the day it reached the bookshops and, although the second edition was of sixty thousand copies, it was exhausted almost as quickly. I believe the book ran into forty-five editions before the early demand had ceased. Naturally, there have been a number of soft-cover editions through the years. But I feel that Lorelei's accomplishments reached a peak when she became one of the few contemporary authors to be represented in the Oxford Book of Quotations.

Following its American publication, Gentlemen Prefer Blondes became a bestseller in thirteen languages. (Note to Khrushchev: Where are my royalties, Tovarich?) In China the story ran as a serial in the newspaper edited by Lin Yutang, who assured me that Lorelei's prose went quite normally into the vernacular of the Sing Song girls.

The world and its ways have changed a great deal since Lorelei Lee made her first appearance on the scene. Recently during a television interview in London, the question was put to me: 'Miss Loos, your book was based on an economic situation, the unparalleled prosperity of the twenties. If you were to write such a book today, what would be your theme?' And without hesitation, I was forced to answer, 'Gentlemen Prefer Gentlemen' (a statement which brought the session abruptly to a close). But if that fact is true, as it very well seems to be, it, too, is based soundly on economics, the criminally senseless population explosion which a beneficent Nature is trying to curb by more pleasant means than war.

So now my little book passes on as a period piece to the grandchildren of its first readers. And, if their spirits should need bolstering, as they cower in the bomb shelters of the sixties, may they be diverted by the adventures of Lorelei Lee and take courage in the words of her favorite philosopher: 'Smile, smile, smile.'

Anita Loos, 1963

Gentlemen Prefer Blondes

Chapter One

March 16th

A gentleman friend and I were dining at the Ritz last evening
and he said that if I took a pencil and a paper and put down all of
my thoughts it would make a book. This almost made me smile
as what it would really make would be a whole row of encyc-
lopediacs. I mean I seem to be thinking practically all of the
time. I mean it is my favorite recreation and sometimes I sit for
hours and do not seem to do anything else but think. So this
gentleman said a girl with brains ought to do something else with
them besides think. And he said he ought to know brains when
he sees them, because he is in the senate and he spends quite a
great deal of time in Washington, dc, and when he comes into
contract with brains he always notices it. So it might have all
blown over but this morning he sent me a book. And so when my
maid brought it to me, I said to her, 'Well, Lulu, here is another
book and we have not read half the ones we have got yet.' But
when I opened it and saw that it was all a blank I remembered
what my gentleman acquaintance said, and so then I realized
that it was a diary. So here I am writing a book instead of reading
one.

But now it is the 16th of March and of course it is to late to
begin with January, but it does not matter as my gentleman
friend, Mr Eisman, was in town practically all of January and

February, and when he is in town one day seems to be practically the same as the next day.

I mean Mr Eisman is in the wholesale button profession in Chicago and he is the gentleman who is known practically all over Chicago as Gus Eisman the Button King. And he is the gentleman who is interested in educating me, so of course he is always coming down to New York to see how my brains have improved since the last time. But when Mr Eisman is in New York we always seem to do the same thing and if I wrote down one day in my diary, all I would have to do would be to put quotation marks for all other days. I mean we always seem to have dinner at the Colony and see a show and go to the Trocadero and then Mr Eisman shows me to my apartment. So of course when a gentleman is interested in educating a girl, he likes to stay and talk about the topics of the day until quite late, so I am quite fatigued the next day and I do not really get up until it is time to dress for dinner at the Colony.

It would be strange if I turn out to be an authoress. I mean at my home near Little Rock, Arkansas, my family all wanted me to do something about my music. Because all of my friends said I had talent and they all kept after me and kept after me about practising. But some way I never seemed to care so much about practising. I mean I simply could not sit for hours and hours at a time practising just for the sake of a career. So one day I got quite tempermental and threw the old mandolin clear across the room and I have really never touched it since. But writing is different because you do not have to learn or practise and it is more tempermental because practising seems to take all the temperment out of me. So now I really almost have to smile because I have just noticed that I have written clear across two pages onto March 18th, so this will do for today and tomorrow. And it just shows how tempermental I am when I get started.

March 19th

Well last evening Dorothy called up and Dorothy said she has met a gentleman who gave himself an introduction to her in the lobby of the Ritz. So then they went to luncheon and tea and dinner and then they went to a show and then they went to the Trocadero. So Dorothy said his name was Lord Cooksleigh but what she really calls him is Coocoo. So Dorothy said why don't you and I and Coocoo go to the Follies tonight and bring Gus along if he is in town? So then Dorothy and I had quite a little quarrel because every time that Dorothy mentions the subject of Mr Eisman she calls Mr Eisman by his first name, and she does not seem to realize that when a gentleman who is as important as Mr Eisman, spends quite a lot of money educating a girl, it really does not show reverance to call a gentleman by his first name. I mean I never even think of calling Mr Eisman by his first name, but if I want to call him anything at all, I call him 'Daddy' and I do not even call him 'Daddy' if a place seems to be public. So I told Dorothy that Mr Eisman would not be in town until day after tomorrow. So then Dorothy and Coocoo came up and we went to the Follies.

So this morning Coocoo called up and he wanted me to luncheon at the Ritz. I mean these foreigners really have quite a nerve. Just because Coocoo is an Englishman and a Lord he thinks a girl can waste hours on him just for a luncheon at the Ritz, when all he does is talk about some exposition he went on to a place called Tibet and after talking for hours I found out that all they were was a lot of chinamen. So I will be quite glad to see Mr Eisman when he gets in. Because he always has something quite interesting to talk about, as for instants the last time he was here he presented me with quite a beautiful emerald bracelet. So next week is my birthday and he always has some delightful surprise on holidays.

I did intend to luncheon at the Ritz with Dorothy today and of course Coocoo had to spoil it, as I told him that I could not luncheon with him today, because my brother was in town on business and had the mumps, so I really could not leave him alone. Because of course if I went to the Ritz now I would bump into Coocoo. But I sometimes almost have to smile at my own imagination, because of course I have not got any brother and I have not even thought of the mumps for years. I mean it is no wonder that I can write.

So the reason I thought I would take luncheon at the Ritz was because Mr Chaplin is at the Ritz and I always like to renew old acquaintances, because I met Mr Chaplin once when we were both working on the same lot in Hollywood and I am sure he would remember me. Gentlemen always seem to remember blondes. I mean the only career I would like to be besides an authoress is a cinema star and I was doing quite well in the cinema when Mr Eisman made me give it all up. Because of course when a gentleman takes such a friendly interest in educating a girl as Mr Eisman does, you like to show that you appreciate it, and he is against a girl being in the cinema because his mother is authrodox.

March 20th

Mr Eisman gets in tomorrow to be here in time for my birthday. So I thought it would really be delightful to have at least one good time before Mr Eisman got in, so last evening I had some literary gentlemen in to spend the evening because Mr Eisman always likes me to have literary people in and out of the apartment. I mean he is quite anxious for a girl to improve her mind and his greatest interest in me is because I always seem to want to improve my mind and not waste any time. And Mr Eisman likes me to have what the French people call a 'salo' which means that people all get together in the evening and improve their minds. So I invited all of the brainy gentlemen I could think up. So I thought up a gentleman who is the proffessor of all of the economics up at Columbia College, and the editor who is the famous editor of the New York Transcript and another gentleman who is a famous playright who writes very, very famous plays that are all about Life. I mean anybody would recognize his name but it always seems to slip my memory because all of us real friends of his only call him Sam. So Sam asked if he could bring a gentleman who writes novels from England, so I said yes, so he brought him. And then we all got together and I called up Gloria and Dorothy and the gentlemen brought their own liquor. So of course the place was a wreck this morning and Lulu and I worked like proverbial dogs to get it cleaned up, but Heaven knows how long it will take to get the chandelier fixed.

March 22nd

Well my birthday has come and gone but it was really quite depressing. I mean it seems to me a gentleman who has a friendly interest in educating a girl like Gus Eisman, would want her to have the biggest square cut diamond in New York. I mean I must say I was quite disappointed when he came to the apartment with a little thing you could hardly see. So I told him I thought it was quite cute, but I had quite a headache and I had better stay in a dark room all day and I told him I would see him the next day, perhaps. Because even Lulu thought it was quite small and she said, if she was I, she really would do something definite and she said she always believed in the old addage, 'Leave them while you're looking good.' But he came in at dinner time with really a very very beautiful bracelet of square cut diamonds so I was quite cheered up. So then we had dinner at the Colony and we went to a show and supper at the Trocadero as usual whenever he is in town. But I will give him credit that he realized how small it was. I mean he kept talking about how bad business was and the button profession was full of bolshevicks who make nothing but trouble. Because Mr Eisman feels that the country is really on the verge of the bolshevicks and I become quite worried. I mean if the bolshevicks do get in, there is only one gentleman who could handle them and that is Mr D. W. Griffith. Because I will never forget when Mr Griffith was directing Intolerance. I mean it was my last cinema just before Mr Eisman made me give up my career and I was playing one of the girls that fainted at the battle when all of the gentlemen fell off the tower. And when I saw how Mr Griffith handled all of those mobs in Intolerance I realized that he could do anything, and I really think that the government of America ought to tell Mr Griffith to get all ready if the bolshevicks start to do it.

Well I forgot to mention that the English gentleman who writes novels seems to have taken quite an interest in me, as soon as he found out that I was literary. I mean he has called up every day and I went to tea twice with him. So he has sent me a whole complete set of books for my birthday by a gentleman called Mr Conrad. They all seem to be about ocean travel although I have not had time to more than glance through them. I have always liked novels about ocean travel ever since I posed for Mr Christie for the front cover of a novel about ocean travel by McGrath because I always say that a girl never really looks as well as she does on board a steamship, or even a yacht.

So the English gentleman's name is Mr Gerald Lamson as those who have read his novels would know. And he also sent me some of his own novels and they all seem to be about middle age English gentlemen who live in the country over in London and seem to ride bicycles, which seems quite different from America, except at Palm Beach. So I told Mr Lamson how I write down all of my thoughts and he said he knew I had something to me from the first minute he saw me and when we become better acquainted I am going to let him read my diary. I mean I even told Mr Eisman about him and he is quite pleased. Because of course Mr Lamson is quite famous and it seems Mr Eisman has read all of his novels going to and fro on the trains and Mr Eisman is always anxious to meet famous people and take them to the Ritz to dinner on Saturday night. But of course I did not tell Mr Eisman that I am really getting quite a little crush on Mr Lamson, which I really believe I am, but Mr Eisman thinks my interest in him is more literary.

March 30th

At last Mr Eisman has left on the 20th Century and I must say I am quite fatigued and a little rest will be quite welcome. I mean I do not mind staying out late every night if I dance, but Mr Eisman is really not such a good dancer so most of the time we just sit and drink some champagne or have a bite to eat and of course I do not dance with anyone else when I am out with Mr Eisman. But Mr Eisman and Gerry, as Mr Lamson wants me to call him, became quite good friends and we had several evenings, all three together. So now that Mr Eisman is out of town at last, Gerry and I are going out together this evening and Gerry said not to dress up, because Gerry seems to like me more for my soul. So I really had to tell Gerry that if all the gentlemen were like he seems to be, Madame Frances' whole dress making establishment would have to go out of business. But Gerry does not like a girl to be nothing else but a doll, but he likes her to bring in her husband's slippers every evening and make him forget what he has gone through.

But before Mr Eisman went to Chicago he told me that he is going to Paris this summer on professional business and I think he intends to present me with a trip to Paris as he says there is nothing so educational as traveling. I mean it did worlds of good to Dorothy when she went abroad last spring and I never get tired of hearing her telling how the merry-go-rounds in Paris have pigs instead of horses. But I really do not know whether to be thrilled or not because, of course, if I go to Paris I will have to leave Gerry and both Gerry and I have made up our minds not to be separated from one another from now on.

March 31st

Last night Gerry and I had dinner at quite a quaint place where we had roast beef and baked potato. I mean he always wants me to have food which is what he calls 'nourishing', which most gentlemen never seem to think about. So then we took a hansom cab and drove for hours around the park because Gerry said the air would be good for me. It is really very sweet to have some one think of all those things that gentlemen hardly ever seem to think about. So then we talked quite a lot. I mean Gerry knows how to draw a girl out and I told him things that I really would not even put in my diary. So when he heard all about my life he became quite depressed and we both had tears in our eyes. Because he said he never dreamed a girl could go through so much as I, and come out so sweet and not made bitter by it all. I mean Gerry thinks that most gentlemen are brutes and hardly ever think about a girl's soul.

So it seems that Gerry has had quite a lot of trouble himself and he can not even get married on account of his wife. He and she have never been in love with each other but she was a suffragette and asked him to marry her, so what could he do? So we rode all around the park until quite late talking and philosophizing quite a lot and I finally told him that I thought, after all, that bird life was the highest form of civilization. So

Gerry calls me his little thinker and I really would not be surprised if all of my thoughts will give him quite a few ideas for his novels. Because Gerry says he has never seen a girl of my personal appearance with so many brains. And he had almost given up looking for his ideal when our paths seemed to cross each other and I told him I really thought a thing like that was nearly always the result of fate.

So Gerry says that I remind him quite a lot of Helen of Troy, who was of Greek extraction. But the only Greek I know is a Greek gentleman by the name of Mr Georgopolis who is really quite wealthy and he is what Dorothy and I call a 'Shopper' because you can always call him up at any hour and ask him to go shopping and he is always quite delighted, which very few gentlemen seem to be. And he never seems to care how much anything costs. I mean Mr Georgopolis is also quite cultured, as I know quite a few gentlemen who can speak to a waiter in French but Mr Georgopolis can also speak to a waiter in Greek which very few gentlemen seem to be able to do.

April 1st

I am taking special pains with my diary from now on as I am really writing for Gerry. I mean he and I are going to read it together some evening in front of the fireplace. But Gerry leaves this evening for Boston as he has to lecture about all of his works at Boston, but he will rush right back as soon as possible. So I am going to spend all of my time improving myself while he is gone. And this afternoon we are both going to a museum on 5th Avenue, because Gerry wants to show me a very very beautiful cup made by an antique jeweler called Mr Cellini and he wants me to read Mr Cellini's life which is a very very fine book and not dull while he is in Boston.

So the famous playright friend of mine who is called Sam called up this morning and he wanted me to go to a literary party tonight that he and some other literary gentlemen are giving to Florence Mills in Harlem but Gerry does not want me to go with Sam as Sam always insists on telling riskay stories. But personally I am quite broad minded and I always say that I do not mind a riskay story as long as it is really funny. I mean I have a great sense of humor. But Gerry says Sam does not always select and choose his stories and he just as soon I did not go out with him. So I am going to stay home and read the book by Mr Cellini instead, because, after all, the only thing I am really interested in, is improving my mind. So I am going to do nothing else but improve my mind while Gerry is in Boston. I mean I just received a cable from Willie Gwynn who arrives from Europe tomorrow, but I am not even going to bother to see him. He is a sweet boy but he never gets anywhere and I am not going to waste my time on such as him, after meeting a gentleman like Gerry.

April 2nd

I seem to be quite depressed this morning as I always am when there is nothing to put my mind to. Because I decided not to read the book by Mr Cellini. I mean it was quite amuseing in spots because it was really quite riskay but the spots were not so close together and I never seem to like to always be hunting clear through a book for the spots I am looking for, especially when there are really not so many spots that seem to be so amuseing after all. So I did not waste my time on it but this morning I told Lulu to let all of the house work go and spend the day reading a book entitled 'Lord Jim' and then tell me all about it, so that I would improve my mind while Gerry is away. But when I got her the book I nearly made a mistake and gave her a book by the title of 'The Nigger of the Narcissus' which really would have hurt her feelings. I mean I do not know why authors cannot say 'Negro' instead of 'Nigger' as they have their feelings just the same as we have.

Well I just got a telegram from Gerry that he will not be back until tomorrow and also some orchids from Willie Gwynn, so I may as well go to the theatre with Willie tonight to keep from getting depressed, as he really is a sweet boy after all. I mean he never really does anything obnoxious. And it is quite depressing to stay at home and do nothing but read, unless you really have a book that is worth bothering about.

April 3rd

I was really so depressed this morning that I was even glad to get a letter from Mr Eisman. Because last night Willie Gwynn came to take me to the Follies, but he was so intoxicated that I had to telephone his club to send around a taxi to take him home. So that left me alone with Lulu at nine o'clock with nothing to do, so I put in a telephone call for Boston to talk to Gerry but it never went through. So Lulu tried to teach me how to play mah jong, but I really could not keep my mind on it because I was so depressed. So today I think I had better go over to Madame Frances and order some new evening gowns to cheer me up.

Well Lulu just brought me a telegram from Gerry that he will be in this afternoon, but I must not meet him at the station on account of all of the reporters who always meet him at the station wherever he comes from. But he says he will come right up to see me as he has something to talk about.

April 4th

What an evening we had last evening. I mean it seems that Gerry is madly in love with me. Because all of the time he was in Boston lecturing to the womens clubs he said, as he looked over the faces of all those club women in Boston, he never realized I was so beautiful. And he said that there was only one in all the world and that was me. But it seems that Gerry thinks that Mr Eisman is terrible and that no good can come of our friendship. I mean I was quite surprised, as they both seemed to get along quite well together, but it seems that Gerry never wants me to see Mr Eisman again. And he wants me to give up everything and study French and he will get a divorce and we will be married. Because Gerry does not seem to like the kind of life all of us lead in New York and he wants me to go home to papa in Arkansas and he will send me books to read so that I will not get lonesome there. And he gave me his uncle's Masonic ring, which came down from the time of Soloman and which he never even lets his wife wear, for our engagement ring, and this afternoon a lady friend of his is going to bring me a new system she thought up of how to learn French. But some way I still seem to be depressed. I mean I could not sleep all night thinking of the terrible things Gerry said about New York and about Mr Eisman. Of course I can understand Gerry being jealous of any gentleman friend of mine and of course I never really thought that Mr Eisman was Rudolph Valentino, but Gerry said it made him cringe to think of a sweet girl like I having a friendship with Mr Eisman. So it really made me feel quite depressed. I mean Gerry likes to talk quite a lot and I always think a lot of talk is depressing and worries your brains with things you never even think of when you are busy. But so long as Gerry does not mind me going out with other gentlemen when they have something to give you mentally, I am going to luncheon with Eddie Goldmark of the Goldmark Films who is always wanting me to sign a contract to go into the cinema. Because Mr Goldmark is madly in love with Dorothy and Dorothy is always wanting me to go back in the cinema because Dorothy says that she will go if I will go.

April 6th

Well I finally wrote Mr Eisman that I was going to get married and it seems that he is coming on at once as he would probably like to give me his advice. Getting married is really quite serious and Gerry talks to me for hours and hours about it. I mean he never seems to get tired of talking and he does not seem to even want to go to shows or dance or do anything else but talk, and if I don't really have something definite to put my mind on soon I will scream.

April 7th

Well Mr Eisman arrived this morning and he and I had quite a long talk, and after all I think he is right. Because here is the first real opportunity I have ever really had. I mean to go to Paris and broaden out and improve my writing, and why should I give it up to marry an author, where he is the whole thing and all I would be would be the wife of Gerald Lamson? And on top of that I would have to be dragged into the scandal of a divorce court and get my name smirched. So Mr Eisman said that opportunities come to seldom in a girls life for me to give up the first one I have really ever had. So I am sailing for France and London on Tuesday and taking Dorothy with me and Mr Eisman says that he will see us there later. So Dorothy knows all of the ropes and she can get along in Paris just as though she knew French and besides she knows a French gentleman who was born and raised there, who speaks it like a native and knows Paris like a book. And Dorothy says that when we get to London nearly everybody speaks English anyway. So it is quite lucky that Mr Lamson is out lecturing in Cincinnati and he will not be back until Wednesday and I can send him a letter and tell him that I have to go to Europe now but I will see him later perhaps. So anyway I will be spared listening to any more of his depressing conversation. So Mr Eisman gave me quite a nice string of pearls and he gave Dorothy a diamond pin and we all went to the Colony for dinner and we all went to a show and supper at the Trocadero and we all spent quite a pleasant evening.

Fate Keeps on Happening

Chapter Two

April 11th

Well Dorothy and I are really on the ship sailing to Europe as anyone could tell by looking at the ocean. I always love the ocean. I mean I always love a ship and I really love the *Majestic* because you would not know it was a ship because it is just like being at the Ritz, and the steward says the ocean is not so obnoxious this month as it generally is. So Mr Eisman is going to meet us next month in Paris because he has to be there on business. I mean he always says that there is really no place to see the latest styles in buttons like Paris.

So Dorothy is out taking a walk up and down the deck with a gentleman she met on the steps, but I am not going to waste my time going around with gentlemen because if I did nothing but go around I would not finish my diary or read good books which I am always reading to improve my mind. But Dorothy really does not care about her mind and I always scold her because she does nothing but waste her time by going around with gentlemen who do not have anything, when Eddie Goldmark of the Goldmark Films is really quite wealthy and can make a girl delightful presents. But she does nothing but waste her time and yesterday, which was really the day before we sailed, she would not go to luncheon with Mr Goldmark but she went to luncheon to meet a gentleman called Mr Mencken from Baltimore who really only prints a green magazine which has not even got any pictures in it. But Mr Eisman is always saying that every girl does not want to get ahead and get educated like me.

So Mr Eisman and Lulu come down to the boat to see me off and Lulu cried quite a lot. I mean I really believe she could not care any more for me if she was light and not colored. Lulu has had a very sad life because when she was quite young a pullman porter fell madly in love with her. So she believed him and he lured her away from her home to Ashtabula and deceived her there. So she finally found out that she had been deceived and she really was broken hearted and when she tried to go back home she found out that it was to late because her best girl friend, who she had always trusted, had stolen her husband and he would not take Lulu back. So I have always said to her she could always work for me and she is going to take care of the apartment until I get back, because I would not sublet the apartment because Dorothy sublet her apartment when she went to Europe last year and the gentleman who sublet the apartment allowed girls to pay calls on him who were not nice.

Mr Eisman has literally filled our room with flowers and the steward has had quite a hard time to find enough vases to put them into. I mean the steward said he knew as soon as he saw Dorothy and I that he would have quite a heavy run on vases. And of course Mr Eisman has sent me quite a lot of good books as he always does, because he always knows that good books are always welcome. So he has sent me quite a large book of Etiquette as he says there is quite a lot of Etiquette in England and London and it would be a good thing for a girl to learn. So I am going to take it on the deck after luncheon and read it, because I would often like to know what a girl ought to do when a gentleman she has just met, says something to her in a taxi. Of course I always become quite vexed but I always believe in giving a gentleman another chance.

So now the steward tells me it is luncheon time, so I will go upstairs as the gentleman Dorothy met on the steps has invited us to luncheon in the Ritz, which is a special dining room on the ship where you can spend quite a lot of money because they really give away the food in the other dining room.

April 12th

I am going to stay in bed this morning as I am quite upset as I saw a gentleman who quite upset me. I am not really sure it was the gentleman, as I saw him a quite a distants in the bar, but if it really is the gentleman it shows that when a girl has a lot of fate in her life it is sure to keep on happening. So when I thought I saw this gentleman I was with Dorothy and Major Falcon, who is the gentleman Dorothy met on the steps, and Major Falcon noticed that I became upset, so he wanted me to tell him what was the matter, but it is really so terrible that I would not want to tell anyone. So I said good night to Major Falcon and I left him with Dorothy and I went down to our room and did nothing but cry and send the steward for some champagne to cheer me up. I mean champagne always makes me feel philosophical because it makes me realize that when a girl's life is as full of fate as mine seems to be, there is nothing else to do about it. So this morning the steward brought me my coffee and quite a large pitcher of ice water so I will stay in bed and not have any more champagne until luncheon time.

Dorothy never has any fate in her life and she does nothing but waste her time and I really wonder if I did right to bring her with me and not Lulu. I mean she really gives gentlemen a bad impression as she talks quite a lot of slang. Because when I went up yesterday to meet she and Major Falcon for luncheon, I overheard her say to Major Falcon that she really liked to become intoxicated once in a 'dirty' while. Only she did not say intoxicated, but she really said a slang word that means intoxicated and I am always having to tell her that 'dirty' is a slang word and she really should not say 'dirty'.

Major Falcon is really quite a delightful gentleman for an Englishman. I mean he really spends quite a lot of money and we had quite a delightful luncheon and dinner in the Ritz until I thought I saw the gentleman who upset me and I am so upset I think I will get dressed and go up on the deck and see if it really is the one I think it is. I mean there is nothing else for me to do as I have finished writing in my diary for today and I have decided not to read the book of Ettiquette as I glanced through it and it does not seem to have anything in it that I would care to know because it wastes quite a lot of time telling you what to call a Lord and all the Lords I have met have told me what to call them and it is generally some quite cute name like Coocoo whose real name is really Lord Cooksleigh. So I will not waste my time on such a book. But I wish I did not feel so upset about the gentleman I think I saw.

April 13th

It really is the gentleman I thought I saw. I mean when I found out it was the gentleman my heart really stopped. Because it all brought back things that anybody does not like to remember, no matter who they are. So yesterday when I went up on the deck to see if I could see the gentleman and see if it really was him, I met quite a delightful gentleman who I met once at a party called Mr Ginzberg. Only his name is not Mr Ginzberg any more because a gentleman in London called Mr Battenburg, who is some relation to some king, changed his name to Mr Mountbatten which Mr Ginzberg says really means the same thing after all. So Mr Ginzberg changed his name to Mr Mountginz which he really thinks is more aristocratic. So we walked around the deck and we met the gentleman face to face and I really saw it was him and he really saw it was me. I mean his face became so red it was almost a picture. So I was so upset I said good-bye to Mr. Mountginz and I started to rush right down to my room and cry. But when I was going down the steps, I bumped right into Major Falcon who noticed that I was upset. So Major Falcon made me go to the Ritz and have some champagne and tell him all about it.

So then I told Major Falcon about the time in Arkansas when Papa sent me to Little Rock to study how to become a stenographer. I mean Papa and I had quite a little quarrel because Papa did not like a gentleman who used to pay calls on me in the park and Papa thought it would do me good to get away for awhile. So I was in the business colledge in Little Rock for about a week when a gentleman called Mr Jennings paid a call on the business colledge because he wanted to have a new stenographer. So he looked over all we colledge girls and he picked me out. So he told our teacher that he would help me finish my course in his office because he was only a lawyer and I really did not have to know so much. So Mr Jennings helped me quite a lot and I stayed in his office about a year when I found out he was not the kind of a gentleman that a young girl is safe with. I mean one evening when I went to pay a call on him at his apartment, I found a girl there who really was famous all over Little Rock for not being nice. So when I found out that girls like that paid calls on Mr Jennings I had quite a bad case of hysterics and my mind was really a blank and when I came out of it, it seems that I had a revolver in my hand and it seems that the revolver had shot Mr Jennings.

So this gentleman on the boat was really the District Attorney who was at the trial and he really was quite harsh at the trial and he called me names that I would not even put in my diary. Because everyone at the trial except the District Attorney was really lovely to me and all the gentlemen in the jury all cried when my lawyer pointed at me and told them that they practically all had had either a mother or a sister. So the jury was only out three minutes and then they came back and acquitted me and they were all so lovely that I really had to kiss all of them and when I kissed the judge he had tears in his eyes and he took me right home to his sister. I mean it was when Mr Jennings became shot that I got the idea to go into the cinema, so Judge Hibbard got me a ticket to Hollywood. So it was Judge Hibbard who really gave me my name because he did not like the name I had because he said a girl ought to have a name that ought to express her personality. So he said my name ought to be Lorelei which is the name of a girl who beeame famous for sitting on a rock in Germany. So I was in Hollywood in the cinema when I met Mr Eisman and he said that a girl with my brains ought not to be in the cinema but she ought to be educated, so he took me out of the cinema so he could educate me.

So Major Falcon was really quite interested in everything I talked about, because he said it was quite a co-instance because this District Attorney, who is called Mr Bartlett, is now working for the government of America and he is on his way to a place called Vienna on some business for Uncle Sam that is quite a great secret and Mr Falcon would like very much to know what the secret is, because the Government in London sent him to America especially to find out what it was. Only of course Mr Bartlett does not know who Major Falcon is, because it is such a great secret, but Major Falcon can tell me, because he knows who he can trust. So Major Falcon says he thinks a girl like I ought to forgive and forget what Mr Bartlett called me and he wants to bring us together and he says he thinks Mr Bartlett would talk to me quite a lot when he really gets to know me and I forgive him for that time in Little Rock. Because it would be quite romantic for Mr Bartlett and I to become friendly, and gentlemen who work for Uncle Sam generally like to become romantic with girls. So he is going to bring us together on the deck after dinner tonight and I am going to forgive him and talk with him quite a lot, because why should a girl hold a grudge against a gentleman who had to do it. So Major Falcon brought me quite a large bottle of perfume and a quite cute imitation of quite a large size dog in the little shop which is on board the boat. I mean Major Falcon really knows how to cheer a girl up quite a lot and so tonight I am going to make it all up with Mr Bartlett.

April 14th

Well Mr Bartlett and I made it all up last night and we are going to be the best of friends and talk quite a lot. So when I went down to my room quite late Major Falcon came down to see if I and Mr Bartlett were really going to be friends because he said a girl with brains like I ought to have lots to talk about with a gentleman with brains like Mr Bartlett who knows all of Uncle Sam's secrets.

So I told Major Falcon how Mr Bartlett thinks that he and I seem to be like a play, because all the time he was calling me all those names in Little Rock he really thought I was. So when he found out that I turned out not to be, he said he always thought that I only used my brains against gentlemen and really had quite a cold heart. But now he thinks I ought to write a play about how he called me all those names in Little Rock and then, after seven years, we became friendly.

So I told Major Falcon that I told Mr Bartlett I would like to write the play but I really did not have time as it takes quite a lot of time to write my diary and read good books. So Mr Bartlett did not know that I read books which is quite a co-instance because he reads them to. So he is going to bring me a book of philosophy this afternoon called 'Smile, Smile, Smile' which all the brainy senators in Washington are reading which cheers you up quite a lot.

So I told Major Falcon that having a friendship with Mr Bartlett was really quite enervating because Mr Bartlett does not drink anything and the less anybody says about his dancing the better. But he did ask me to dine at his table, which is not in the Ritz and I told him I could not, but Major Falcon told me I ought to, but I told Major Falcon that there was a limit to almost everything. So I am going to stay in my room until luncheon and I am going to luncheon in the Ritz with Mr. Mountginz who really knows how to treat a girl.

Dorothy is up on the deck wasting quite a lot of time with a gentleman who is only a tennis champion. So I am going to ring for the steward and have some champagne which is quite good for a person on a boat. The steward is really quite a nice boy and he has had quite a sad life and he likes to tell me all about himself. I mean it seems that he was arrested in Flatbush because he promised a gentleman that he would bring him some very very good scotch and they mistook him for a bootlegger. So it seems they put him in a prison and they put him in a cell with two other gentlemen who were very, very famous burglars. I mean they really had their pictures in all the newspapers and everybody was talking about them. So my steward, whose real name is Fred, was very very proud to be in the same cell with such famous burglars. So when they asked him what he was in for, he did not like to tell them that he was only a bootlegger, so he told them that he set fire to a house and burned up quite a large family in Oklahoma. So, everything would have gone alright except that the police had put a dictaphone in the cell and used it all against him and he could not get out until they had investigated all the fires in Oklahoma. So I always think that it is much more educational to talk to a boy like Fred who has been through a lot and really suffered than it is to talk to a gentleman like Mr Bartlett. But I will have to talk to Mr Bartlett all afternoon as Major Falcon has made an appointment for me to spend the whole afternoon with him.

April 15th

Last night there was quite a maskerade ball on the ship which was really all for the sake of charity because most of the sailors seem to have orphans which they get from going on the ocean when the sea is very rough. So they took up quite a collection and Mr Bartlett made quite a long speech in favor of orphans especially when their parents are sailors. Mr Bartlett really likes to make speeches quite a lot. I mean he even likes to make speeches when he is all alone with a girl when they are walking up and down a deck. But the maskerade ball was quite cute and one gentleman really looked almost like an imitation of Mr Chaplin. So Dorothy and I really did not want to go to the ball but Mr Bartlett bought us two scarfs at the little store which is on the ship so we tied them around our hips and everyone said we made quite a cute Carmen. So Mr Bartlett and Major Falcon and the tennis champion were the Judges. So Dorothy and I won the prizes. I mean I really hope I do not get any more large size imitations of a dog as I have three now and I do not see why the Captain does not ask Mr Cartier to have a jewelry store on the ship as it is really not much fun to go shopping on a ship with gentlemen, and buy nothing but imitations of dogs.

So after we won the prizes I had an engagement to go up on the top of the deck with Mr Bartlett as it seems he likes to look at the moonlight quite a lot. So I told him to go up and wait for me and I would be up later as I promised a dance to Mr Mountginz. So he asked me how long I would be dancing till, but I told him to wait up there and he would find out. So Mr Mountginz and I had quite a delightful dance and champagne until Major Falcon found us. Because he was looking for me and he said I really should not keep Mr Bartlett waiting. So I went up on the deck and Mr Bartlett was up there waiting for me and it seems that he really is madly in love with me because he did not sleep a wink since we became friendly. Because he never thought that I really had brains but now that he knows it, it seems that he has been looking for a girl like me for years, and he said that really the place for me when he got back home was Washington dc where he lives. So I told him I thought a thing like that was nearly always the result of fate. So he wanted me to get off the ship tomorrow at France and take the same trip that he is taking to Vienna as it seems that Vienna is in France and if you go on to England you go to far. But I told him that I could not because I thought that if he was really madly in love with me he would take a trip to London instead. But he told me that he had serious business in Vienna that was a very, very great secret. But I told him I did not believe it was business but that it really was some girl, because what business could be so important? So he said it was business for the United States government at Washington and he could not tell anybody what it was. So then we looked at the moonlight quite a lot. So I told him I would go to Vienna if I really knew it was business and not some girl, because I could not see how business could be so important. So then he told me all about it. So it seems that Uncle Sam wants some new aeroplanes that everybody else seems to want, especially England, and Uncle Sam has quite a clever way to get them which is to long to put in my diary. So we sat up and saw the sun rise and I became quite stiff and told I would have to go down to my room because, after all, the ship lands at France today and I said if I got off the boat at France to go to Vienna with him I would have to pack up.

So I went down to my room and went to bed. So then Dorothy came in and she was up on the deck with the tennis champion but she did not notice the sun rise as she really does not love nature but always wastes her time and ruins her clothes even though I always tell her not to drink champagne out of a bottle on the deck of the ship as it lurches quite a lot. So I am going to have luncheon in my room and I will send a note to Mr Bartlett to tell him I will not be able to get off the boat at France to go to Vienna with him as I have quite a headache, but I will see him sometime somewhere else. So Major Falcon is going to come down at 12 and I have got to thinking over what Mr Bartlett called me at Little Rock and I am quite upset. I mean a gentleman never pays for those things but a girl always pays. So think I will tell Major Falcon all about the airoplane business as he really wants to know. And, after all I do not think Mr Bartlett is a gentleman to call me all those names in Little Rock even if it was seven years ago. I mean Major Falcon is always a gentleman and he really wants to do quite a lot for us in London. Because he knows the Prince of Wales and he thinks that Dorothy and I would like the Prince of Wales once we had really got to meet him. So I am going to stay in my room until Mr Bartlett gets off the ship at France, because I really do not seem to care if I never see Mr Bartlett again.

So tomorrow we will be at England bright and early. And I really feel quite thrilled because Mr Eisman sent me a cable this morning, as he does every morning, and he says to take advantage of everybody we meet as traveling is the highest form of education. I mean Mr Eisman is always right and Major Falcon knows all the sights in London including the Prince of Wales so it really looks like Dorothy and I would have quite a delightful time in London.

London Is Really Nothing

Chapter Three

April 17th

Well, Dorothy and I are really at London. I mean we got to London on the train yesterday as the boat does not come clear up to London but it stops on the beach and you have to take a train. I mean everything is much better in New York, because the boat comes right up to New York and I am really beginning to think that London is not so educational after all. But I did not tell Mr Eisman when I cabled him last night because Mr Eisman really sent me to London to get educated and I would hate to tell him that London is a failure because we know more in New York.

So Dorothy and I came to the Ritz and it is delightfully full of Americans. I mean you would really think it was New York because I always think that the most delightful thing about traveling is to always be running into Americans and to always feel at home.

So yesterday Dorothy and I went down to luncheon at the Ritz and we saw a quite cute little blond girl at the next table and I nudged Dorothy under the table, because I do not think it is nice to nudge a person on top of the table as I am trying to teach good manners to Dorothy. So I said 'That is quite a cute little girl so she must be an American girl.' And sure enough she called the headwaiter with quite an American accent and she was quite angry and she said to him, I have been coming to this hotel for 35 years and this is the first time I have been kept waiting. So I recognized her voice because it was really Fanny Ward. So we asked her to come over to our table and we were all three delighted to see each other. Because I and Fanny have known each other for about five years but I really feel as if I knew her better because mamma knew her 45 years ago when she and mamma used to go to school together and mamma used to always follow all her weddings in all the newspapers. So now Fanny lives in London and is famous for being one of the cutest girls in London. I mean Fanny is almost historical, because when a girl is cute for 50 years it really begins to get historical.

So if mamma did not die of hardening of the arterys she and Fanny and I could have quite a delightful time in London as Fanny loves to shop. So we went shopping for hats and instead of going to the regular shop we went to the childrens department and Fanny and I bought some quite cute hats as childrens hats only cost half as much and Fanny does it all the time. I mean Fanny really loves hats and she buys some in the children's department every week, so she really saves quite a lot of money.

So we came back to the Ritz to meet Major Falcon because Major Falcon invited us to go to tea with him at a girls house called Lady Shelton. So Major Falcon invited Fanny to go with us to, but she was sorry because she had to go to her music lesson.

So at Lady Sheltons house we met quite a few people who seemed to be English. I mean some of the girls in London seem to be Ladies which seems to be the opposite of a Lord. And some who are not Ladies are honorable. But quite a few are not Ladies or honorable either, but are just like us, so all you have to call them is 'Miss'. So Lady Shelton was really delighted to have we Americans come to her house. I mean she took Dorothy and I into the back parlor and tried to sell us some shell flowers she seems to make out of sea shells for 25 pounds. So we asked her how much it was in money and it seems it is 125 dollars. I mean I am really going to have a quite hard time in London with Dorothy because she really should not say to an English lady what she said. I mean she should not say to an English lady that in America we use shells the same way only we put a dry pea under one of them and we call it a game. But I told Lady Shelton we really did not need any shell flowers. So Lady Shelton said she knew we Americans loved dogs so she would love us to meet her mother.

So then she took Dorothy and Major Falcon and I to her mother's house which was just around the corner from her house. Because her mother seems to be called a Countess and raise dogs. So her mother was having a party too, and she seemed to have quite red hair and quite a lot of paint for such an elderly lady. So the first thing she asked us was she asked us if we bought some shell flowers from her daughter. So we told her no. But she did not seem to act like a Countess of her elderly age should act. Because she said, 'You were right my dears – don't let my daughter stick you – they fall apart in less than a week.' So then she asked us if we would like to buy a dog. I mean I could not stop Dorothy but she said 'How long before the dogs fall apart?' But I do not think the Countess acted like a Countess ought to act because she laughed very, very loud and she said that Dorothy was really priceless and she grabed Dorothy and kissed her and held her arm around her all the time. I mean I really think that a Countess should not encouradge Dorothy or else she is just as unrefined as Dorothy seems to be. But I told the Countess that we did not need any dog.

So then I met quite a delightful English lady who had a very, very beautiful diamond tiara in her hand bag because she said that she thought some Americans would be at the party and it was really a very, very great bargain. I mean I think a diamond tiara is delightful because it is a place where I really never thought of wearing diamonds before, and I thought I had almost one of everything until I saw a diamond tiara. The English lady who is called Mrs Weeks said it was in her family for years but the good thing about diamonds is they always look new. So I was really very intreeged and I asked her how much it cost in money and it seems it was $7,500.

So then I looked around the room and I noticed a gentleman who seemed to be quite well groomed. So I asked Major Falcon who he was and he said he was called Sir Francis Beekman and it seems he is very, very wealthy. So then I asked Major Falcon to give us an introduction to one another and we met one another and I asked Sir Francis Beekman if he would hold my hat while I could try on the diamond tiara because I could wear it backwards with a ribbon, on account of my hair being hobbled, and I told Sir Francis Beekman that I really thought it looked quite cute. So he thought it did to, but he seemed to have another engagement. So the Countess came up to me and she is really very unrefined because she said to me 'Do not waste your time on him' because she said that whenever Sir Francis Beekman spent a haypenny the statue of a gentleman called Mr Nelson took off his hat and bowed. I mean some people are so unrefined they seem to have unrefined thoughts about everything.

So I really have my heart set on the diamond tiara and I became quite worried because Mrs Weeks said she was going to a delightful party last night that would be full of delightful Americans and it would be snaped up. So I was so worried that I gave her 100 dollars and she is going to hold the diamond tiara for me. Because what is the use of traveling if you do not take advantage of oportunities and it really is quite unusual to get a bargain from an English lady. So last night I cabled Mr Eisman and I told Mr Eisman that he does not seem to know how much it costs to get educated by traveling and I said I really would have to have $10,000 and I said I hoped I would not have to borrow the money from some strange English gentleman, even if he might be very very good looking. So I really could not sleep all night because of all my worrying because if I do not get the money to buy the diamond tiara it may be a quite hard thing to get back $100 from an English lady.

So now I must really get dressed as Major Falcon is going to take Dorothy and I to look at all the sights in London. But I really think if I do not get the diamond tiara my whole trip to London will be quite a failure.

April 18th

Yesterday was quite a day and night. I mean Major Falcon came to take Dorothy and I to see all the sights in London. So I thought it would be delightful if we had another gentleman and I made Major Falcon call up Sir Francis Beekman. I mean I had a cable from Mr Eisman which told me he could not send me 10,000 dollars but he would send me 1000 dollars which really would not be a drop in the bucket for the diamond tiara. So Sir Francis Beekman said that he could not come but I teased him and teased him over the telephone so he finally said he would come.

So Major Falcon drives his own car so Dorothy sat with him and I sat with Sir Francis Beekman but I told him that I was not going to call him Sir Francis Beekman but I was really going to call him Piggie.

In London they make a very, very great fuss over nothing at all. I mean London is really nothing at all. For instants, they make a great fuss over a tower that really is not even as tall as the Hickox building in Little Rock Arkansas and it would only make a chimney on one of our towers in New York. So Sir Francis Beekman wanted us to get out and look at the tower because he said that quite a famous Queen had her head cut off there one morning and Dorothy said, 'What a fool she was to get up that morning' and that is really the only sensible thing that Dorothy has said in London. So we did not bother to get out.

So we did not go to any more sights because they really have delicious champagne cocktails at a very very smart new restaurant called the Cafe de Paris that you could not get in New York for either love nor money and I told Piggie that when you are traveling you really ought to take advantadges of what you can not do at home.

So while Dorothy and I were in the Cafe de Paris powdering our nose in the lady's dressing room we met an American girl who Dorothy knew in the Follies, but now she is living in London. So she told us all about London. So it seems the gentlemen in London have quite a quaint custom of not giving a girl many presents. I mean the English girls really seem to be satisfied with a gold cigaret holder or else what they call a 'bangle' which means a bracelet in English which is only gold and does not have any stones in it which American girls would really give to their maid. So she said you could tell what English gentlemen were like when you realize that not even English ladys could get anything out of them. So she said Sir Francis Beekman was really famous all over London for not spending so much money as most English gentlemen. So then Dorothy and I said goodbye to Dorothy's girl friend and Dorothy said, 'Lets tell our two boy friends that we have a headache and go back to the Ritz, where men are Americans.' Because Dorothy said that the society of a gentleman like Sir Francis Beekman was to great a price to pay for a couple of rounds of champagne cocktails. But I told Dorothy that I always believe that there is nothing like trying and I think it would be nice for an American girl like I to educate an English gentleman like Piggie, as I call Sir Francis Beekman.

So then we went back to the table and I almost have to admit that Dorothy is in the right about Piggie because he really likes to talk quite a lot and he is always talking about a friend of his who was quite a famous King in London called King Edward. So Piggie said he would never never forget the jokes King Edward was always saying and he would never forget one time they were all on a yacht and they were all sitting at a table and

King Edward got up and said, 'I don't care what you gentlemen do – I'm going to smoke a cigar.' So then Piggie laughed very, very loud. So of course I laughed very, very loud and I told Piggie he was wonderful the way he could tell jokes. I mean you can always tell when to laugh because Piggie always laughs first.

So in the afternoon a lot of lady friends of Mrs Weeks heard about me buying the diamond tiara and called us up and asked us to their house to tea so Dorothy and I went and we took a gentleman Dorothy met in the lobby who is very, very good looking but he is only an English ballroom dancer in a cafe when he has a job.

So we went to tea to a lady's house called Lady Elmsworth and what she has to sell we Americans seems to be a picture of her father painted in oil paint who she said was a whistler. But I told her my own father was a whistler and used to whistle all of the time and I did not even have a picture of him but every time he used to go to Little Rock I asked him to go to the photographers but he did not go.

So then we met a lady called Lady Chizzleby that wanted us to go to her house to tea but we told her that we really did not want to buy anything. But she said that she did not have anything to sell but she wanted to borrow five pounds. So we did not go and I am really glad that Mr Eisman did not come to London as all the English ladys would ask him to tea and he would have a whole ship load of shell flowers and dogs and anteek pictures that do nobody any good.

So last night Piggie and I and Dorothy and the dancer who is called Gerald went to the Kit Kat Club as Gerald had nothing better to do because he is out of a job. So Dorothy and I had quite a little quarrel because I told Dorothy that she was wasting quite a lot of time going with any gentleman who is out of a job but Dorothy is always getting to really like somebody and she will never learn how to act. I mean I always seem to think that when a girl really enjoys being with a gentleman, it puts her to quite a disadvantage and no real good can come of it.

Well tonight is going to be quite a night because Major Falcon is going to take Dorothy and I to a dance at a lady's house tonight to meet the Prince of Wales. And now I must get ready to see Piggie because he and I seem to be getting to be quite good friends even if he has not sent me any flowers yet.

April 19th

Last night we really met the Prince of Wales. I mean Major
Falcon called for Dorothy and I at eleven and took us to a ladys
house where the lady was having a party. The Prince of Wales is
really wonderful. I mean even if he was not a prince he would be
wonderful, because even if he was not a prince, he would be able
to make his living playing the ukelele, if he had a little more
practice. So the lady came up to me and told me that the Prince
of Wales would like to meet me, so she gave us an introduction to
one another and I was very very thrilled when he asked me for a
dance. So I decided I would write down every word he said to
me in my diary so I could always go back and read it over and
over when I am really old. So then we started to dance and I
asked him if he was still able to be fond of horses, and he said he
was. So after our dance was all over he asked Dorothy for a
dance but Dorothy will never learn how to act in front of a
prince. Because she handed me her fan and she said 'Hold this
while I slip a new page into English histry,' right in front of the
Prince of Wales. So I was very very worried while Dorothy was
dancing with the Prince of Wales because she talked to the
Prince of Wales all the time and when she got through the Prince
of Wales wrote some of the slang words she is always saying on
his cuff, so if he tells the Queen some day to be 'a good Elk' or

65

some other slang word Dorothy is always saying, the Queen will really blame me for bringing such a girl into English society. So when Dorothy came back we had quite a little quarrel because Dorothy said that since I met the Prince of Wales I was becoming too English. But really, I mean to say, I often remember papa back in Arkansas and he often used to say that his grandpa came from a place in England called Australia, so really, I mean to say, it is no wonder that the English seems to come out of me sometimes. Because if a girl seems to have an English accent I really think it is quite jolly.

April 20th

Yesterday afternoon I really thought I ought to begin to educate Piggie how to act with a girl like American gentlemen act with a girl. So I asked him to come up to have tea in our sitting room in the hotel because I had quite a headache. I mean I really look quite cute in my pink negligay. So I sent out a bell hop friend of Dorothy and I who is quite a nice boy who is called Harry and who we talk to quite a lot. So I gave Harry ten pounds of English money and I told him to go to the most expensive florist and to buy some very very expensive orchids for 10 pounds and to bring them to our sitting room at fifteen minutes past five and not to say a word but to say they were for me. So Piggie came to tea and we were having tea when Harry came in and he did not say a word but he gave me a quite large box and he said it was for me. So I opened the box and sure enough they were a dozen very very beautiful orchids. So I looked for a card, but of course there was no card so I grabbed Piggie and I said I would have to give him quite a large hug because it must have been him. But he said it was not him. But I said it must be him because I said that there was only one gentleman in London who was so sweet and generous and had such a large heart to send a girl one dozen orchids like him. So he still said it was not him. But I said I knew it was him, because there was not a gentleman in London so really marvelous and so wonderful and such a marvelous gentleman to send a girl one dozen orchids every day as him. So I really had to apologize for giving him such a large hug but I told him I was so full of impulses that when I knew he was going to send me one dozen orchids every day I became so impulsive I could not help it!

So then Dorothy and Gerald came in and I told them all about what a wonderful gentleman Piggie turned out to be and I told them when a gentleman sent a girl one dozen orchids every day he really reminded me of a prince. So Piggie blushed quite a lot and he was really very very pleased and he did not say any more that it was not him. So then I started to make a fuss over him and I told him he would have to look out because he was really so good looking and I was full of impulses that I might even lose my mind some time and give him a kiss. So Piggie really felt very very good to be such a good looking gentleman. So he could not help blushing all the time and he could not help grinning all the time from one ear to another. So he asked us all to dinner and then he and Gerald went to change their clothes for dinner. So Dorothy and I had quite a little quarrel after they went because Dorothy asked me which one of the Jesse James brothers was my father. But I told her I was not so unrefined that I would waste my time with any gentleman who was only a ballroom dancer when he had a job. So Dorothy said Gerald was a gentleman because he wrote her a note and it had a crest. So I told her to try and eat it. So then we had to get dressed.

So this morning Harry, the boy friend of ours who is the bell hop, waked me up at ten o'clock because he had a box of one dozen orchids from Piggie. So by the time Piggie pays for a few dozen orchids, the diamond tiara will really seem like quite a bargain. Because I always think that spending money is only just a habit and if you get a gentleman started on buying one dozen orchids at a time he really gets very good habits.

April 21st

Well, yesterday afternoon I took Piggie shopping on a street called Bond Street. So I took him to a jewelry store because I told him I had to have a silver picture frame because I had to have a picture of him to go in it. Because I told Piggie that when a girl gets to know such a good looking gentleman as him she really wants to have a picture of him on her dressing table where she can look at it a lot. So Piggie became quite intreeged. So we looked at all the silver picture frames. But then I told him that I really did not think a silver picture frame was good enough for a picture of him because I forgot that they had gold picture frames until I saw them. So then we started to look at the gold picture frames. So then it came out that his picture was taken in his unaform. So I said he must be so good looking in his unaform that I really did not think even the gold picture frames were good enough but they did not have any platinum picture frames so we had to buy the best one we could.

So then I asked him if he could put on his unaform tomorrow because I would love to see him in his unaform and we could go to tea at Mrs Weeks. So he really became very pleased because he grinned quite a lot and he said that he would. So then I said that poor little I would really look like nothing at all to be going out with him in his georgous unaform. So then we started to look at some bracelets but a lady friend of his who is quite friendly with his wife, who is in their country house in the country, came in to the store, so Piggie became quite nervous to be caught in a jewelery store where he has not been for years and years, so we had to go out.

This morning Gerald called up Dorothy and he said that day after tomorrow they are having a theatrical garden party to sell things to people for charity so he asked if Dorothy and I would be one of the ones who sells things to people for charity. So we said we would.

So now I must telephone Mrs Weeks and say I will bring Sir Francis Beekman to tea tomorrow and I hope it all comes out all right. But I really wish Piggie would not tell so many storys. I mean I do not mind a gentleman when he tells a great many storys if they are new, but a gentleman who tells a great many storys and they are all the same storys is quite enervating. I mean London is really so uneducational that all I seem to be learning is some of Piggies storys and I even want to forget them. So I am really becoming jolly well fed up with London.

April 22nd

Yesterday Piggie came in his unaform but he was really quite upset because he had a letter. I mean his wife is coming to London because she always comes to London every year to get her old clothes made over as she has a girl who does it very very cheap. So she is going to stay with the lady who saw us in the jewelery store, because it always saves money to stay with a friend. So I wanted to cheer Piggie up so I told him that I did not think the lady saw us and if she did see us, she really could not believe her eyes to see him in a jewelery store. But I did not tell him that I think that Dorothy and I had better go to Paris soon. Because, after all, Piggie's society is beginning to tell on a girl's nerves. But I really made Piggie feel quite good about his unaform because I told him I only felt fit to be with him in a diamond tiara. So then I told him that, even if his wife was in London, we could still be friends because I could not help but admire him even if his wife was in London and I told him I really thought a thing like that was nearly always the result of fate. So then we went to tea at Mrs Weeks. So Piggie arranged with Mrs Weeks to pay her for the diamond tiara and she nearly fell dead but she will keep it a secret because no one would believe it anyway. So now I have the diamond tiara and I have to admit that everything always turns out for the best. But

I promised Piggie that I would always stay in London and we would always be friendly. Because Piggie always says that I am the only one who admires him for what he really is.

April 25th

Well, we were so busy the last days I did not have time to write in my diary because now we are on a ship that seems to be quite a small ship to be sailing to Paris and we will be at Paris this afternoon. Because it does not take nearly so long to come to Paris as it does to come to London. I mean it seems quite unusual to think that it takes 6 days to come to London and only one day to come to Paris.

So Dorothy is quite upset because she did not want to come as she is madly in love with Gerald and Gerald said that we really ought not to leave London without going to see England while we happened to be here. But I told him that if England was the same kind of a place that London seems to be, I really know to much to bother with such a place. I mean we had quite a little quarrel because Gerald showed up at the station with a bangle for Dorothy so I told Dorothy she was well rid of such a person. So Dorothy had to come with me because Mr Eisman is paying her expenses because he wants Dorothy to be my chaperone.

So the last thing in London was the garden party. I sold quite a lot of red baloons and I sold a red baloon to Harry Lauder the famous Scotch gentleman who is the famous Scotch tenor for 20 pounds. So Dorothy said I did not need to buy any ticket to

Paris on the boat because if I could do that, I could walk across the channel.

So Piggy does not know that we have gone but I sent him a letter and told him I would see him some time again some time. And I was really glad to get out of our rooms at the Ritz – I mean 50 or 60 orchids really make a girl think of a funeral. So I cabled Mr Eisman and I told him we could not learn anything in London because we knew to much, so if we went to Paris at least we could learn French, if we made up our mind to it.

So I am really very very intreeged as I have heard so much about Paris and I feel that it must be much more educational than London and I can hardly wait to see the Ritz hotel in Paris.

Paris Is Devine

Chapter Four

April 27th

Paris is devine. I mean Dorothy and I got to Paris yesterday, and it really is devine. Because the French are devine. Because when we were coming off the boat, and we were coming through the customs, it was quite hot and it seemed to smell quite a lot and all the French gentlemen in the customs, were squealing quite a lot. So I looked around and I picked out a French gentleman who was really in a very gorgeous uniform and he seemed to be a very, very important gentleman and I gave him twenty francs worth of French money and he was very very gallant and he knocked everybody else down and took our bags right through the custom. Because I really think that twenty Francs is quite cheap for a gentleman that has got on at least $100 worth of gold braid on his coat alone, to speak nothing of his trousers.

I mean the French gentlemen always seem to be squealing quite a lot, especially taxi drivers when they only get a small size yellow dime called a 'fifty santeems' for a tip. But the good thing about French gentlemen is that every time a French gentleman starts in to squeal, you can always stop him with five francs, no matter who he is. I mean it is so refreshing to listen to a French gentleman stop squeaking, that it would really be quite a bargain even for ten francs.

So we came to the Ritz Hotel and the Ritz Hotel is devine. Because when a girl can sit in a delightful bar and have delicious champagne cocktails and look at all the important French people in Paris, I think it is devine. I mean when a girl can sit there and look at the Dolly sisters and Pearl White and Maybelle Gilman Corey, and Mrs Nash, it is beyond worlds. Because when a girl looks at Mrs Nash and realizes what Mrs Nash has got out of gentlemen, it really makes a girl hold her breath.

And when a girl walks around and reads all of the signs with all of the famous historical names it really makes you hold your breath. Because when Dorothy and I went on a walk, we only walked a few blocks but in only a few blocks we read all of the famous historical names, like Coty and Cartier and I knew we were seeing something educational at last and our whole trip was not a failure. I mean I really try to make Dorothy get educated and have reverance. So when we stood at the corner of a place called the Place Vendome, if you turn your back on a monument they have in the middle and look up, you can see none other than Coty's sign. So I said to Dorothy, does it not really give you a thrill to realize that that is the historical spot where Mr Coty makes all the perfume? So then Dorothy said that she supposed Mr Coty came to Paris and he smelled Paris and he realized that something had to be done. So Dorothy will really never have any reverance.

So then we saw a jewelry store and we saw some jewelry in the window and it really seemed to be a very very great bargain but the price marks all had francs on them and Dorothy and I do not seem to be mathematical enough to tell how much francs is in money. So we went in and asked and it seems it was only 20 dollars and it seems it is not diamonds but it is a thing called 'paste' which is the name of a word which means imitations. So Dorothy said 'paste' is the name of the word a girl ought to do to a gentleman that handed her one. I mean I would really be embarrassed, but the gentleman did not seem to understand Dorothy's english.

So it really makes a girl feel depressed to think a girl could not tell that it was nothing but an imitation. I mean a gentleman could deceeve a girl because he could give her a present and it would only be worth 20 dollars. So when Mr Eisman comes to Paris next week, if he wants to make me a present I will make him take me along with him because he is really quite an inveteran bargain hunter at heart. So the gentleman at the jewelry store said that quite a lot of famous girls in Paris had imitations of all their jewelry and they put the jewelry in the safe and they really wore the imitations, so they could wear it and have a good time. But I told him I thought that any girl who was a lady would not even think of having such a good time that she did not remember to hang on to her jewelry.

So then we went back to the Ritz and unpacked our trunks with the aid of really a delightful waiter who brought us up some delicious luncheon and who is called Leon and who speaks english almost like an American and who Dorothy and I talk to quite a lot. So Leon said that we ought not to stay around the Ritz all of the time, but we really ought to see Paris. So Dorothy said she would go down in the lobby and meet some gentleman to show us Paris. So in a couple of minutes she called up on the telephone from the lobby and she said 'I have got a French bird down here who is a French title nobleman, who is called a veecount so come on down.' So I said 'How did a Frenchman get into the Ritz.' So Dorothy said 'He came in to get out of the rain and he has not noticed that it is stopped.' So I said 'I suppose you have picked up something without taxi fare as usual. Why did you not get an American gentleman who always have money?' So Dorothy said she thought a French gentleman had ought to know Paris better. So I said 'He does not even know it is not raining.' But I went down.

So the veecount was really delightful after all. So then we rode around and we saw Paris and we saw how devine it really is. I mean the Eyefull Tower is devine and it is much more educational than the London Tower, because you can not even see the London Tower if you happen to be two blocks away. But when a girl looks at the Eyefull Tower she really knows she is looking at something. And it would even be very difficult not to notice the Eyefull Tower.

So then we went to a place called the Madrid to tea and it

really was devine. I mean we saw the Dolly Sisters and Pearl White and Mrs Corey and Mrs Nash all over again.

So then we went to dinner and then we went to Momart and it really was devine because we saw them all over again. I mean in Momart they have genuine American jazz bands and quite a lot of New York people which we knew and you really would think you were in New York and it was devine. So we came back to the Ritz quite late. So Dorothy and I had quite a little quarrel because Dorothy said that when we were looking at Paris I asked the French veecount what was the name of the unknown soldier who is buried under quite a large monument. So I said I really did not mean to ask him, if I did, because what I did mean to ask him was, what was the name of his mother because it is always the mother of a dead soldier that I always seem to think about more than the dead soldier that has died.

So the French veecount is going to call up in the morning but I am not going to see him again. Because French gentlemen are really quite deceeving. I mean they take you to quite cute places and they make you feel quite good about yourself and you really seem to have a delightful time but when you get home and come to think it all over, all you have got is a fan that only cost 20 francs and a doll that they gave you away for nothing in a restaurant. I mean a girl has to look out in Paris, or she would have such a good time in Paris that she would not get anywheres. So I really think that American gentlemen are the best after all, because kissing your hand may make you feel very very good but a diamond and safire bracelet lasts forever. Besides, I do not think that I ought to go out with any gentlemen in Paris because Mr Eisman will be here next week and he told me that the only kind of gentlemen he wants me to go out with are intelectual gentlemen who are good for a girls brains. So I really do not seem to see many gentlemen around the Ritz who seem to look like they would be good for a girl's brains. So tomorrow we are going to go shopping and I suppose it would really be to much to expect to find a gentleman who would look to Mr Eisman like he was good for a girls brains and at the same time he would like to take us shopping.

April 29th

Yesterday was quite a day. I mean Dorothy and I were getting ready to go shopping and the telephone rang and they said that Lady Francis Beekman was down stairs and she wanted to come up stairs. So I really was quite surprised. I mean I did not know what to say, so I said all right. So then I told Dorothy and then we put our brains together. Because it seems that Lady Francis Beekman is the wife of the gentleman called Sir Francis Beekman who was the admirer of mine in London who seemed to admire me so much that he asked me if he could make me a present of a diamond tiara. So it seemed as if his wife must have heard about it, and it really seemed as if she must have come clear over from London about it. So there was a very very loud knock at the door so we asked her to come in. So Lady Francis Beekman came in and she is a quite large size lady who seems to resemble Bill Hart quite a lot. I mean Dorothy thinks that Lady Francis Beekman resembles Bill Hart quite a lot, only she really thinks she looks more like Bill Hart's horse. So it seems that she said that if I did not give her back the diamond tiara right away, she would make quite a fuss and she would ruin my reputation. Because she said that something really must be wrong about the whole thing. Because it seems that Sir Francis Beekman and she have been married for 35 years and the last present he gave to her was a wedding ring. So Dorothy spoke up and she said, 'Lady you could no more ruin my girl friends reputation than you could sink the Jewish fleet.' I mean I was quite proud of Dorothy the way she stood up for my reputation. Because I really think that there is nothing so wonderful as two girls when they stand up for each other and help each other a lot. Because no matter how vigarous Lady Francis Beekman seems to be, she had to realize that she could not sink a whole fleet full of ships. So she had to stop talking against my reputation.

So then she said she would drag it into the court and she would say that it was undue influence. So I said to her, 'If you wear that hat into a court, we will see if the judge thinks it took an undue influence to make Sir Francis Beekman look at a girl.' So then Dorothy spoke up and Dorothy said 'My girl friend is right, Lady. You have got to be the Queen of England to get away with a hat like that.' So Lady Francis Beekman seemed to get quite angry. So then she said she would send for Sir Francis Beekman where he suddenly went to Scotland, to go hunting when he found out that Lady Francis Beekman had found out. So Dorothy said 'Do you mean that you have left Sir Francis Beekman loose with all those spendthrifts down in Scotland?' So Dorothy said she would better look out or he would get together with the boys some night and simply massacre a hay-penny. I mean I always encouradge Dorothy to talk quite a lot when we are talking to unrefined people like Lady Francis Beekman, because Dorothy speaks their own languadge to unrefined people better than a refined girl like I. So Dorothy said, 'You had better not send for Sir Francis Beekman because if my girl friend really wanted to turn loose on Sir Francis Beekman, all he would have left would be his title.' So then I spoke right up and said Yes that I was an American girl and we American girls do not care about a title because we American girls always say that what is good enough for Washington is good enough for us. So Lady Francis Beekman really seemed to get more angry and more angry all of the time.

So then she said that if it was necessary, she would tell the judge that Sir Francis Beekman went out of his mind when he gave it to me. So Dorothy said 'Lady, if you go into a court and if the judge gets a good look at you, he will think that Sir Francis Beekman was out of his mind 35 years ago.' So then Lady Francis Beekman said she knew what kind of a person she had to deal with and she would not deal with any such a person because she said it hurt her dignity. So Dorothy said, 'Lady, if we hurt your dignity like you hurt our eyesight I hope for your sake, you are a Christian science.' So that seemed to make Lady Francis Beekman angry. So she said she would turn it all over to her soliciter. So when she went out she tripped over quite a long train which she had on her skirt and she nearly fell down. So Dorothy leaned out of the door and Dorothy called down the hall and said, 'Take a tuck in that skirt Isabel, its 1925.' So I really felt quite depressed because I felt as if our whole morning was really very unrefined just because we had to mix with such an unrefined lady as Lady Francis Beekman.

April 30th

So sure enough yesterday morning Lady Francis Beekman's
solicitor came. Only he really was not a solicitor, but his name
was on a card and it seems his name is Mons. Broussard and it
seems that he is a advocat because an advocat is a lawyer in the
French landguage. So Dorothy and I were getting dressed and
we were in our negligay a usual when there was quite a loud
knock on the door and before we could even say come in he
jumped right into the room. So it seems that he is of French
extraction. I mean Lady Francis Beekman's solicitor can really
squeal just like a taxi driver. I mean he was squealing quite loud
when he jumped into the room and he kept right on squealing.
So Dorothy and I rushed into the parlor and Dorothy looked at
him and Dorothy said, 'This town has got to stop playing jokes
on us every morning' because our nerves could not stand it. So
Mons. Broussard handed us his card and he squealed and
squealed and he really waved his arms in the air quite a lot. So
Dorothy said He gives quite a good imitation of the Moulan
Rouge, which is really a red wind mill, only Dorothy said he
makes more noise and he runs on his own wind. So we stood and
watched him for quite a long while, but he seemed to get quite
monotonous after quite a long while because he was always talking in French, which really means nothing to us. So Dorothy

said 'Lets see if 25 francs will stop him, because if 5 francs will stop a taxi driver, 25 francs ought to stop an advocat.' Because he was making about 5 times as much noise as a taxi driver and 5 times 5 is 25. So as soon as he heard us start in to talk about francs he seemed to calm down quite a little. So Dorothy got her pocket book and she gave him 25 francs. So then he stopped squealing and he put it in his pocket, but then he got out quite a large size handkerchief with purple elefants on it and he started in to cry. So Dorothy really got discouraged and she said, 'Look here, you have given us a quite an amusing morning but if you keep that up much longer, wet or dry, out you go.'

So then he started in to pointing at the telephone and he seemed to want to use the telephone and Dorothy said, 'If you think you can get a number over that thing, go to it, but as far as we have found out, it is a wall bracket.' So then he started in to telephone so Dorothy and I went about our business to get dressed. So when he finished telephoning he kept running to my door and then he kept running to Dorothy's door, and he kept on crying and talking a lot, but he seemed to have lost all of his novelty to us so we paid no more attention to him.

So finally there was another loud knock on the door so we heard him rush to the door so we both went in to the parlor to see what it was and it really was a sight. Because it was another Frenchman. So the new Frenchman rushed in and he yelled Papa and he kissed him. So it seems that it was his son because his son is really his papa's partner in the advocat business. So then his papa talked quite a lot and then he pointed at I and Dorothy. So then his son looked at us and then his son let out quite a large size squeal, and he said in French, 'May papa, elles sont sharmant.' So it seems he was telling his papa in French that we were really charming. So then Mons. Broussard stopped crying and put on his glasses and took a good look at us. So then his son put up the window shade, so his papa could get a better look at us. So when his papa had finished looking at us he really became delighted. So he became all smiles and he pinched our cheeks and he kept on saying Sharmant all of the time because Sharmant means charming in the French languadge. So then his son broke right out into english and he really speaks english as good as an American. So then he told us his papa telephoned for him to come over because we did not seem to understand what his papa was saying to us. So it seems that Mons. Broussard had been talking to us in english all of the time but we did not seem to understand his kind of english. So Dorothy said, 'If what your papa was talking in was english, I could get a gold medal for my greek.' So then his son told his papa and his papa laughed very very loud and he pinched Dorothys cheek and he was very delighted even if the joke was on him. So then Dorothy and I asked his son what he was saying, when he was talking to us in english and his son said he was telling us all about his client, Lady Francis Beekman. So then we asked his son why his papa kept crying. So then his son said his papa kept crying because he was thinking about Lady Francis Beekman. So Dorothy said, 'If he cries when he thinks about her, what does he do when he looks at her?' So then his son explained to his papa what Dorothy said. So then Mons. Broussard laughed very very loud, so then he kissed Dorothy's hand, so he said, after that, we would all really have to have a bottle of champagne. So he went to the telephone and ordered a bottle of champagne.

So then his son said to his papa, 'Why do we not ask the charming ladies to go out to Fountainblo to-day.' So his papa said it would be charming. So then I said, 'How are we going to tell you gentlemen apart, because if it is the same in Paris as it is in America, you would both seem to be Monshure Broussard.' So then we got the idea to call them by their first name. So it seems that his son's name is Louie so Dorothy spoke up and said, 'I hear that they number all of you Louies over here in Paris.' Because a girl is always hearing some one talk about Louie the sixteenth who seemed to be in the anteek furniture business. I mean I was so surprised to hear Dorothy get so historical so she may really be getting educated in spite of everything. But Dorothy told Louie he need not try to figure out his number because she got it the minute she looked at him. So it seems his papa's name is Robber, which means Robert in French. So Dorothy started in to think about her 25 francs and she said to Robber, 'Your mother certainly knew her grammer when she called you that.'

So Dorothy said we might as well go out to Fountainblo with Louie and Robber if Louie would take off his yellow spats that were made out of yellow shammy skin with pink pearl buttons. Because Dorothy said, 'Fun is fun but no girl wants to laugh all of the time.' So Louie is really always anxious to please, so he took off his spats but when he took off his spats, we saw his socks and when we saw his socks we saw that they were Scotch plaid with small size rainbows running through them. So Dorothy looked at them a little while and she really became quite discouraged and she said, 'Well Louie, I think you had better put your spats back on.'

So then Leon, our friend who is the waiter, came in with the bottle of champagne. So while he was opening the bottle of champagne Louie and Robber talked together in French quite a lot and I really think I had ought to find out what they said in French because it might be about the diamond tiara. Because French gentlemen are very very gallant, but I really do not think a girl can trust one of them around a corner. So, when I get a chance, I am going to ask Leon what they said.

So then we went to Fountainblo and then we went to Momart and we got home very late, and we really had quite a delightful day and night, even if we did not go out shopping and buy anything. But I really think we ought to do more shopping because shopping really seems to be what Paris is principaly for.

May 1st

Well this morning I sent for Leon, who is Dorothy and my waiter friend, and I asked him what Louie and Robber said in French. So it seems that they said in French that we seemed to attract them very very much because they really thought that we were very very charming, and they had not met girls that were so charming in quite a long time. So it seems that they said that they would ask us out a lot and that they would charge up all the bills to Lady Francis Beekman because they would watch for their chance and they would steal the diamond tiara. So then they said that even if they could not steal it from us, we were really so charming that it would be delightful to go around with us, even if they could not steal from us. So no matter what happens they really could not lose. Because it seems that Lady Francis Beekman would be glad to pay all the bills when they told her they had to take us out a lot so they could watch for their chance and steal it. Because Lady Francis Beekman is the kind of a wealthy lady that does not spend money on anything else but she will always spend money on a law suit. And she really would not mind spending the money because it seems that something either I or Dorothy said to Lady Francis Beekman seemed to make her angry.

So then I decided it was time to do some thinking and I really thought quite a lot. So I told Dorothy I thought I would put the real diamond tiara in the safe at the Ritz and then I would buy an imitation of a diamond tiara at the jewelry store that has the imitations that are called paste. So then I would leave the imitation of the diamond tiara lying around, so Louie and Robber could see how careless I seem to be with it so then they would get full of encouradgement. So when we go out with Louie and Robber I could put it in my hand bag and I could take it with me so Louie and Robber could always feel that the diamond tiara was within reach. So then Dorothy and I could get them to go shopping and we could get them to spend quite a lot and every time they seemed to get discouradged, I could open my hand bag, and let them get a glimpse of the imitation of a diamond tiara and they would become more encouradged and then they would spend some more money. Because I even might let them steal it at the last, because they were really charming gentlemen after all I really would like to help Louie and Robber. I mean it would be quite amusing for them to steal it for Lady Francis Beekman and she would have to pay them quite a lot and then she would find out it was only made of paste after all. Because Lady Francis Beekman has never seen the real diamond tiara and the imitation of a diamond tiara would really deceive her, at least until Louie and Robber got all of their money for all of the hard work they did. I mean the imitation of a diamond tiara would only cost about 65 dollars and what is 65 dollars if Dorothy and I could do some delightful shopping and get some delightful presents that would even seem more delightful when we stopped to realize that Lady Francis Beekman paid for them. And it would teach Lady Francis Beekman a lesson not to say what she said to two American girls like I and Dorothy, who were all alone in Paris and had no gentlemen to protect them.

So when I got through telling Dorothy what I thought up, Dorothy looked at me and looked at me and she really said she thought my brains were a miracle. I mean she said my brains reminded her of a radio because you listen to it for days and days and you get discouradged and just when you are getting ready to smash it, something comes out that is a masterpiece.

So then Louie called us up so Dorothy told him that we

thought it would be delightful if he and Robber would take us out shopping tomorrow morning. So then Louie asked his papa and his papa said they would. So then they asked us if we would like to go to see a play called The Foley Bergere tonight. So he said that all of the French people who live in Paris are always delighted to have some Americans, so it will give them an excuse to go to the Foley Bergere. So we said we would go. So now Dorothy and I are going out shopping to buy the imitation of a diamond tiara and we are going out window shopping to pick out where we would like Louie and Robber to take us shopping tomorrow.

So I really think that everything always works out for the best. Because after all, we really need some gentlemen to take us around until Mr Eisman gets to Paris and we could not go around with any really attractive gentlemen because Mr Eisman only wants me to go out with gentlemen that have brains. So I said to Dorothy that, even if Louie and Robber do not look so full of brains, we could tell Mr Eisman that all we were learning from them was French. So even if I have not seemed to learn French yet, I have really almost learned to understand Robbers english so when Robber talks in front of Mr Eisman and I seem to understand what he is saying, Mr Eisman will probably think I know French.

May 2nd

So last night we went to the Foley Bergere and it really was devine. I mean it was very very artistic because it had girls in it that were in the nude. So one of the girls was a friend of Louie and he said that she was a very very nice girl, and that she was only 18 years of age. So Dorothy said, 'She is slipping it over on you Louie, because how could a girl get such dirty knees in only 18 years?' So Louie and Robber really laughed very very loud. I mean Dorothy was very unrefined at the Foley Bergere. But I always think that when girls are in the nude it is very artistic and if you have artistic thoughts you think it is beautiful and I really would not laugh in an artistic place like the Foley Bergere.

So I wore the imitation of a diamond tiara to the Foley Bergere. I mean it really would deceeve an expert and Louie and Robber could hardly take their eyes off of it. But they did not really annoy me because I had it tied on very very tight. I mean it would be fatal if they got the diamond tiara before Dorothy and I took them shopping a lot.

So we are all ready to go shopping this morning and Robber was here bright and early and he is in the parlor with Dorothy and we are waiting for Louie. So I left the diamond tiara on the table in the parlor so Robber could see how careless I really am with everything but Dorothy is keeping her eye on Robber. So I just heard Louie come in because I heard him kissing Robber. I mean Louie is always kissing Robber and Dorothy told Louie that if he did not stop kissing Robber, people would think that he painted batiks.

So now I must join the others and I will put the diamond tiara in my hand bag so that Louie and Robber will feel that it is always around and we will all go shopping. And I almost have to smile when I think of Lady Francis Beekman.

May 3rd

Yesterday was really delightful. I mean Louie and Robber bought Dorothy and I some delightful presents. But then they began to run out of all the franks they had with them, so they began to get discouradged but just as soon as they began to get discouradged, I gave Robber my hand bag to hold while I went to the fitting room to try on a blouse. So he was cheered up quite a lot, but of course Dorothy stayed with them and kept her eye on Robber so he did not get a chance. But it really cheered him up quite a lot to even hold it.

So after all their franks were gone, Robber said he would have to telephone to some one, so I suppose he telephoned to Lady Francis Beekman and she must have said All right because Robber left us at a place called the Cafe de la Paix because he had to go on an errand and when he came back from his errand he seemed to have quite a lot more franks. So then they took us to luncheon so that after luncheon we could go out shopping some more.

But I am really learning quite a lot of French in spite of everything. I mean if you want delicious chicken and peas for luncheon all you have to say is 'pettypas' and 'pulley'. I mean French is really very easy, for instance the French use the word 'sheik' for everything, while we only seem to use it for gentlemen when they seem to resemble Rudolf Valentino.

So while we were shopping in the afternoon I saw Louie get Dorothy off in a corner and whisper to her quite a lot. So then I saw Robber get her off in a corner and whisper to her quite a lot. So when we got back to the Ritz, Dorothy told me why they whispered to her. So it seems when Louie whispered to Dorothy, Louie told Dorothy that if she would steal the diamond tiara from me and give it to him and not let his papa know, he would give her 1000 franks. Because it seems that Lady Francis Beekman has got her heart set on it and she will pay quite a lot for it because she is quite angry and when she really gets as angry as she is, she is only a woman with one idea. So if Louie could get it and his papa would not find it out, he could keep all the money for himself. So it seems that later on, when Robber was whispering to Dorothy, he was making her the same proposition for 2000 franks so that Louie would not find out and Robber could keep all the money for himself. So I really think it would be delightful if Dorothy could make some money for herself because it might make Dorothy get some ambishions. So tomorrow morning Dorothy is going to take the diamond tiara and she is going to tell Louie that she stole it and she is going to sell it to Louie. But she will make him hand over the money first and then, just as she is going to hand over the diamond tiara, I am going to walk in on them and say, 'Oh there is my diamond tiara. I have been looking for it everywhere.' So then I will get it back. So then she will tell him that she might just as well keep the 1000 franks because she will steal it for him again in the afternoon. So in the afternoon she is going to sell it to Robber and I really think we will let Robber keep it. Because I am quite fond of Robber. I mean he is quite a sweet old gentleman and it is really refreshing the way he and his son love one another. Because even if it is unusual for an American to see a French gentleman always kissing his father, I really think it is refreshing and I think that we Americans would be better off if we American fathers and sons would love one another more like Louie and Robber.

So Dorothy and I have quite a lot of delightful hand bags and stockings and handkerchiefs and scarfs and things and some quite cute models of evening gowns that are all covered with imitations of diamonds, only they do not call them 'paste' when they are on a dress but they call them 'diamonteys' and I really think a girl looks quite cute when she is covered all over with 'diamonteys'.

May 5th

So yesterday morning Dorothy sold the imitation of a diamond tiara to Louie. So then we got it back. So in the afternoon we all went out to Versigh. I mean Louie and Robber were quite delighted not to go shopping any more so I suppose that Lady Francis Beekman really thinks that there is a limit to almost everything. So I took Louie for a walk at Versigh so that Dorothy would have a chance to sell it to Robber. So then she sold it to Robber. So then he put it in his pocket. But when we were coming home I got to thinking things over and I really got to thinking that an imitation of a diamond tiara was quite a good thing to have after all. I mean especially if a girl goes around a lot in Paris, with admirers who are of the French extraction. And after all, I really do not think a girl ought to encouradge Robber to steal something from two American girls who are all alone in Paris and have no gentlemen to protect them. So I asked Dorothy which pocket Robber put it in, so I sat next to him in the automobile coming home and I took it out.

So we were in quite a quaint restaurant for dinner when Robber put his hand in his pocket and then he started in to squeal once more. So it seems he had lost something, so he and Louie had one of their regular squealing and shoulder shrugging matches. But Louie told his papa that he did not steal it out of his papa's pocket. But then Robber started in to cry to think that his son would steal something out of his own papa's pocket. So after Dorothy and I had had about all we could stand, I told them all about it. I mean I really felt sorry for Robber so I told him not to cry any more because it was nothing but paste after all. So then I showed it to them. So then Louie and Robber looked at Dorothy and I and they really held their breath. So I suppose that most of the girls in Paris do not have such brains as we American girls.

So after it was all over, Louie and Robber seemed to be so depressed that I really felt sorry for them. So I got an idea. So I told them that we would all go out tomorrow to the imitation of a jewelry store and they could buy another imitation of a diamond tiara to give to Lady Francis Beekman and they could get the man in the jewelry store to put on the bill that it was a hand bag and they could charge the bill to Lady Francis Beekman along with the other expenses. Because Lady Francis Beekman had never seen the real diamond tiara anyway. So Dorothy spoke up and Dorothy said that as far as Lady Francis Beekman would know about diamonds, you could nick off a piece of ice and give it to her, only it would melt. So then Robber looked at me and looked at me, and he reached over and kissed me on the forehead in a way that was really full of reverance.

So then we had quite a delightful evening. I mean because we all seem to understand one another because, after all, Dorothy and I could really have a platonick friendship with gentlemen like Louie and Robber. I mean there seems to be something common between us, especially when we all get to thinking about Lady Francis Beekman.

So they are going to charge Lady Francis Beekman quite a lot of money when they give her the imitation of a diamond tiara and I told Robber if she seems to complane to ask her, if she knew that Sir Francis Beekman sent me 10 pounds worth of orchids every day while we were in London. So that would make her so angry that she would be glad to pay almost anything to get the diamond tiara.

So when Lady Francis Beekman pays them all the money, Louie and Robber are going to give us a dinner in our honor at

Ciros. So when Mr Eisman gets here on Saturday, Dorothy and I are going to make Mr Eisman give Louie and Robber a dinner in their honor at Ciros because of the way they helped us when we were two American girls all alone in Paris and could not even speak the French landguage.

So Louie and Robber asked us to come to a party at their sister's house today but Dorothy says we had better not go because it is raining and we both have brand new umbrellas that are quite cute and Dorothy says she would not think of leaving a brand new umbrella in a French lady's hall and it is no fun to hang on to an umbrella all the time you are at a party. So we had better be on the safe side and stay away. So we called up Louie and told him we had a headache but we thanked him for all of his hospitality. Because it is the way all the French people like Louie and Robber are so hospitable to we Americans that really makes Paris so devine.

The Central of Europe

Chapter Five

May 16th

I really have not written in my diary for quite a long time, because Mr Eisman arrived in Paris and when Mr Eisman is in Paris we really do not seem to do practically anything else but the same thing.

I mean we go shopping and we go to a show and we go to Momart and when a girl is always going with Mr Eisman nothing practically happens. And I did not even bother to learn any more French because I always seem to think it is better to leave French to those that can not do anything else but talk French. So finally Mr Eisman seemed to lose quite a lot of interest in all of my shopping. So he heard about a button factory that was for sale quite cheaply in Vienna and as Mr Eisman is in the button profession, he thought it would be a quite good thing to have a button factory in Vienna so he went to Vienna and he said he did not care if he did not ever see the rue de la Paix again. So he said if he thought Vienna would be good for a girl's brains, he would send for Dorothy and I and we could meet him at Vienna and learn something. Because Mr Eisman really wants me to get educated more than anything else, especially shopping.

So now we have a telegram, and Mr Eisman says in the telegram for Dorothy and I to take an oriental express because we really ought to see the central of Europe because we American girls have quite a lot to learn in the central of Europe. So Dorothy says if Mr Eisman wants us to see the central of Europe she bets there is not a rue de la Paix in the whole central of Europe.

So Dorothy and I are going to take an oriental express tomorrow and I really think it is quite unusual for two American girls like I and Dorothy to take an oriental express all alone, because it seems that in the Central of Europe they talk some other kinds of landguages which we do not understand besides French. But I always think that there is nearly always some gentleman who will protect two American girls like I and Dorothy who are all alone and who are traveling in the Central of Europe to get educated.

May 17th

So now we are on an oriental express and everything seems to be quite unusual. I mean Dorothy and I got up this morning and we looked out of the window of our compartment and it was really quite unusual. Because it was farms, and we saw quite a lot of girls who seemed to be putting small size hay stacks onto large size hay stacks while their husbands seemed to sit at a table under quite a shady tree and drink beer. Or else their husbands seemed to sit on a fence and smoke their pipe and watch them. So Dorothy and I looked at two girls who seemed to be ploughing up all of the ground with only the aid of a cow and Dorothy said, 'I think we girls have gone one step to far away from New York, because it begins to look to me as if the Central of Europe is no country for we girls.' So we both became quite worried. I mean I became quite depressed because if this is what Mr Eisman thinks we American girls ought to learn I really think it is quite depressing. So I do not think we care to meet any gentlemen who have been born and raised in the Central of Europe. I mean the more I travel and the more I seem to see other gentlemen the more I seem to think of American gentlemen.

So now I am going to get dressed and go to the dining car and look for some American gentleman and hold a conversation, because I really feel so depressed. I mean Dorothy keeps trying to depress me because she keeps saying that I will probably end up in a farm in the Central of Europe doing a sister act with a plough. Because Dorothy's jokes are really very unrefined and I think that I will feel much better if I go to the dining car and have some luncheon.

Well I went to the dining car and I met a gentleman who was quite a delightful American gentleman. I mean it was quite a co-instance, because we girls have always heard about Henry Spoffard and it was really nobody else but the famous Henry Spoffard, who is the famous Spoffard family, who is a very very fine old family who is very very wealthy. I mean Mr Spoffard is one of the most famous familys in New York and he is not like most gentlemen who are wealthy, but he works all of the time for the good of the others. I mean he is the gentleman who always gets his picture in all of the newspapers because he is always senshuring all of the plays that are not good for peoples morals. And all of we girls remember the time when he was in the Ritz for luncheon and he met a gentleman friend of his and the gentleman friend had Peggy Hopkins Joyce to luncheon and he introduced Peggy Hopkins Joyce to Mr Spoffard and Mr Spoffard turned on his heels and walked away. Because Mr Spoffard is a very very famous Prespyterian and he is really much to Prespyterian to meet Peggy Hopkins Joyce. I mean it is unusual to see a gentleman who is such a young gentleman as Mr Spoffard be so Prespyterian, because when most gentlemen are 35 years of age their minds nearly always seem to be on something else.

So when I saw no one else but the famous Mr Spoffard I really became quite thrilled. Because all of we girls have tried very hard to have an introduction to Henry Spoffard and it was quite unusual to be shut up on a train in the Central of Europe with him. So I thought it would be quite unusual for a girl like I to have a friendship with a gentleman like Mr Spoffard, who really does not even look at a girl unless she at least looks like a Prespyterian. And I mean our family in Little Rock were really not so Prespyterian.

So I thought I would sit at his table. So then I had to ask him about all of the money because all of the money they use in the Central of Europe has not even got so much sense to it as the kind of franks they use in Paris. Because it seems to be called kronens and it seems to take quite a lot of them because it takes 50,000 of them to even buy a small size package of cigarettes and Dorothy says if the cigarettes had tobacco in them, we couldn't lift enough kronens over a counter to pay for a package. So this morning Dorothy and I asked the porter to bring us a bottle of champagne and we really did not know what to give him for a tip. So Dorothy said for me to take one of the things called a one million kronens and she would take one of them called a one million kronens and I would give him mine first and if he gave me quite a dirty look, she would give him hers. So after we paid for the bottle of champagne I gave him my one million kronens and before we could do anything else he started in to grabbing my hand and kissing my hand and getting down on his knees. So we finally had to push him right out of the compartment. So one million kronens seemed to be enough. So I told Mr Spoffard how we did not know what to give the porter when he brought us our bottle of mineral water. So then I asked him to tell me all about all of the money because I told him I always seem to think that a penny earned was a penny saved. So it really was quite unusual because Mr Spoffard said that that was his favorite motto.

So then we got to talking quite a lot and I told him that I was traveling to get educated and I told him I had a girl with me who I was trying to reform because I thought if she would put her mind more on getting educated, she would get more reformed. Because after all Mr Spoffard will have to meet Dorothy sooner or later and he might wonder what a refined girl like I was doing with a girl like Dorothy. So Mr Spoffard really became quite intreeged. Because Mr Spoffard loves to reform people and he loves to senshure everything and he really came over to Europe to look at all the things that Americans come over to Europe to look at, when they really should not look at them but they should look at all of the museums instead. Because if that is all we Americans come to Europe to look at, we should stay home and look at America first. So Mr Spoffard spends all of his time looking at things that spoil peoples morals. So Mr Spoffard really must have very very strong morals or else all the things that spoil other peoples morals would spoil his morals. But they do not seem to spoil Mr Spoffards morals and I really think it is wonderful to have such strong morals. So I told Mr Spoffard that I thought that civilization is not what it ought to be and we really ought to have something else to take its place.

So Mr Spoffard said that he would come to call on Dorothy and I in our compartment this afternoon and we would talk it all over, if his mother does not seem to need him in her compartment. Because Mr Spoffards mother always travels with Mr Spoffard and he never does anything unless he tells his mother all about it, and asks his mother if he ought to. So he told me that that is the reason he has never got married, because his mother does not think that all of the flappers we seem to have nowadays are what a young man ought to marry when a young man is full of so many morals as Mr Spoffard seems to be full of. So I told Mr Spoffard that I really felt just like his mother feels about all of the flappers because I am an old fashioned girl.

So then I got to worrying about Dorothy quite a lot because Dorothy is really not so old-fashioned and she might say something in front of Mr Spoffard that might make Mr Spoffard wonder what such an old-fashioned girl as I was doing with such a girl as Dorothy. So I told him how I was having quite a hard time reforming Dorothy and I would like to have him meet Dorothy so he could tell me if he really thinks I am wasting quite a lot of time trying to reform a girl like Dorothy. So then he had to go to his mother. So I really hope that Dorothy will act more reformed than she usually acts in front of Mr Spoffard.

Well Mr Spoffard just left our compartment so he really came to pay a call on us after all. So Mr Spoffard told us all about his mother and I was really very very intreeged because if Mr Spoffard and I become friendly he is the kind of a gentleman that always wants a girl to meet his mother. I mean if a girl gets to know what kind of a mother a gentlemans mother is like, she really knows more what kind of a conversation to use on a gentleman's mother when she meets her. Because a girl like I is really always on the verge of meeting gentlemen's mothers. But such an unrefined girl as Dorothy is really not the kind of a girl that ever meets gentlemens mothers.

So Mr Spoffard says his mother has to have him take care of her quite a lot. Because Mr Spoffards mothers brains have never really been so strong. Because it seems his mother came from such a very fine old family that even when she was quite a small size child she had to be sent to a school that was a special school for people of very fine old familys who had to have things very easy on their brain. So she still has to have things very easy on her brain, so she has a girl who is called her companion who goes with her everywhere who is called Miss Chapman. Because Mr Spoffard says that there is always something new going on in the world which they did not get a chance to tell her about at the school. So now Miss Chapman keeps telling her instead. Because how would she know what to think about such a new thing as a radio, for instance, if she did not have Miss Chapman to tell her what it was, for instance. So Dorothy spoke up and Dorothy said, 'What a responsibility that girl has got on her shoulders. For instance, what if Miss Chapman told her a radio was something to build a fire in, and she would get cold some day and stuff it full of papers and light it.' But Mr Spoffard told Dorothy that Miss Chapman would never make such a mistake. Because he said that Miss Chapman came from a very very fine old family herself and she really had a fine brain. So Dorothy said, 'If she really has got such a fine brain I bet her fine old family had an ice man who could not be trusted.' So Mr Spoffard and I did not pay any more attention to Dorothy because Dorothy really does not know how to hold a conversation.

So then I and Mr Spoffard held a conversation all about morals and Mr Spoffard says he really thinks the future of everything is between the hands of Mr Blank the district attorney who is the famous district attorney who is closing up all the places in New York where they sell all of the liquor. So Mr Spoffard said that a few months ago, when Mr Blank decided he would try to get the job to be the district attorney, he put 1,000 dollars worth of liquor down his sink. So now Mr Blank says that everybody else has got to put it down their sink. So Dorothy spoke up, and Dorothy said, 'If he poured 1,000 dollars worth down his sink to get himself one million dollars worth of publicity and a good job – when we pour it down our sink, what do we get?' But Mr Spoffard is to brainy a gentleman to answer any such a foolish question. So he gave Dorothy a look that was full of dignity and he said he would have to go back to his Mother. So I was really quite angry at Dorothy. So I followed Mr Spoffard down the hall of the railway train and I asked Mr Spoffard if he thought I was wasting quite a lot of time reforming a girl like Dorothy. So Mr Spoffard thinks I am, because he really thinks a girl like Dorothy will never have any reverance. So I told Mr Spoffard I had wasted so much time on Dorothy it would really break my heart to be a failure. So then I had tears in my eyes. So Mr Spoffard is really very very sympathetic because when he saw that I did not have any handkerchief, he took his own handkerchief and he dried up all of my tears. So then he said he would help me with Dorothy quite a lot and get her mind to running on things that are more educational.

So then he said he thought that we ought to get off the train at a place called Munich because it was very full of art, which they call 'kunst' in Munich, which is very, very educational. So he said he and Dorothy and I would get off the train in Munich because he could send his mother right on to Vienna with Miss Chapman, because every place always seems to look alike to his mother anyway. So we are all going to get off the train at Munich and I can send Mr Eisman a telegram when nobody is looking. Because I really do not think I will tell Mr Spoffard about Mr Eisman, because, after all, their religions are different and when two gentlemen have such different religions they do not seem to have so much to get congeneal about. So I can telegraph Mr Eisman that Dorothy and I thought we would get off the train at Munich to look at all of the art.

So then I went back to Dorothy and I told Dorothy if she did not have anything to say in the future to not say it. Because even if Mr Spoffard is a fine old family and even if he is very Prespyterian, I and he could really be friendly after all and talk together quite a lot. I mean Mr Spoffard likes to talk about himself quite a lot, so I said to Dorothy it really shows that, after all, he is just like any other gentleman. But Dorothy says she would demand more proof than that. So Dorothy says she thinks that maybe I might become quite friendly with Mr Spoffard and especially with his mother because she thinks his mother and I have quite a lot that is common, but she says, if I ever bump into Miss Chapman, she thinks I will come to a kropper because Dorothy saw Miss Chapman when she was at luncheon and Dorothy says Miss Chapman is the kind of a girl that wears a collar and a tie even when she is not on horseback. And Dorothy said it was the look that Miss Chapman gave her at luncheon that really gave her the idea about the ice man. So Dorothy says she thinks Miss Chapman has got 3 thirds of the brains of that trio of Geegans, because Geegans is the slang word that Dorothy has thought up to use on people who are society people. Because Dorothy says she thinks any gentleman with Mr Spoffards brains had ought to spend his time putting nickels into an electric piano, but I did not even bother to talk back at such a girl as Dorothy. So now we must get ready to get off the train when the train gets to Munich so that we can look at all of the kunst in Munich.

May 19th

Well yesterday Mr Spoffard and I and Dorothy got off the train at Munich to see all of the kunst in Munich, but you only call it Munich when you are on the train because as soon as you get off of the train they seem to call it Munchen. So you really would know that Munchen was full of kunst because in case you would not know it, they have painted the word 'kunst' in large size black letters on everything in Munchen, and you can not even see a boot black's stand in Munchen that is not full of kunst.

So Mr Spoffard said that we really ought to go to the theater in Munchen because even the theater in Munchen was full of kunst. So we looked at all of the bills of all of the theaters, with the aid of quite an intelectual hotel clerk who seemed to be able to read it and tell us what it said, because it really meant nothing to us. So it seems they were playing Kiki in Munchen, so I said, let us go and see Kiki because we have seen Lenore Ulric in New York and we would really know what it is all about even if they do not seem to talk the English landguage. So then we went to the Kunst theater. So it seems that Munchen is practically full of Germans and the lobby of the Kunst theater was really full of Germans who stand in the lobby and drink beer and eat quite a lot of Bermudian onions and garlick sausage and hard boiled eggs and beer before all of the acts. So I really had to ask

Mr Spoffard if he thought we had come to the right theater because the lobby seemed to smell such a lot. I mean when the smell of beer gets to be anteek it gets to smell quite a lot. But Mr Spoffard seemed to think that the lobby of the Kunst theatre did not smell any worse than all of the other places in Munich. So then Dorothy spoke up and Dorothy said 'You can say what you want about the Germans being full of "kunst", but what they are really full of is delicatessen'.

So then we went into the Kunst theater. But the Kunst theater does not seem to smell so good as the lobby of the Kunst theater. And the Kunst theater seems to be decorated with quite a lot of what tripe would look like if it was pasted on the wall and gilded. Only you could not really see the gilding because it was covered with quite a lot of dust. So Dorothy looked around and Dorothy said, if this is 'kunst', the art center of the world is Union Hill New Jersey.

So then they started in to playing Kiki but it seems that it was not the same kind of a Kiki that we have in America, because it seemed to be all about a family of large size German people who seemed to keep getting in each others way. I mean when a stage is completely full of 2 or 3 German people who are quite large size, they really cannot help it if they seem to get in each others ways. So then Dorothy got to talking with a young gentleman who seemed to be a German gentleman who sat back of her, who she thought was applauding. But what he was really doing was he was cracking a hard boiled egg on the back of her chair. So he talked English with quite an accent that seemed to be quite a German accent. So Dorothy asked him if Kiki had come out on the stage yet. So he said no, but she was really a beautiful German actress who came clear from Berlin and he said we should really wait until she came out, even if we did not seem to understand it. So finally she came out. I mean we knew it was her because Dorothy's German gentleman friend nudged Dorothy with a sausage. So we looked at her, and we looked at her and Dorothy said, 'If Schuman Heinke still has a grandmother, we have dug her up in Munchen.' So we did not bother to see any more of Kiki because Dorothy said she would really have to know more about the foundations of that building before she would risk our lives to see Kiki do that famous scene where she faints in the last act. Because Dorothy said, if the foundations of that building were as anteek as the smell, there was going to be a catasterophy when Kiki hit the floor. So even Mr Spoffard was quite discouradged, but he was really glad because he said he was 100 per cent of an American and it served the Germans right for starting such a war against all we Americans.

May 20th

Well today Mr Spoffard is going to take me all around to all of the museums in Munchen, which are full of kunst that I really ought to look at, but Dorothy said she had been punished for all of her sins last night, so now she is going to begin life all over again by going out with her German gentleman friend, who is going to take her to a house called the Half Brow house which is the worlds largest size of a Beer Hall. So Dorothy said I could be a high brow and get full of kunst, but she is satisfide to be a Half brow and get full of beer. But Dorothy will really never be full of anything else but unrefinement.

May 21st

Well Mr Spoffard and I and Dorothy are on the train again and
we are all going to Vienna. I mean Mr Spoffard and I spent one
whole day going through all of the museums in Munchen, but I
am really not even going to think about it. Because when something terrible happens to me, I always try to be a Christian
science and I simply do not even think about it, but I deny that
it ever happened even if my feet do seem to hurt quite a lot. So
even Dorothy had quite a hard day in Munchen because her
German gentleman friend, who is called Rudolf, came for her at
11 o'clock to take her to breakfast. But Dorothy told him that
she had had her breakfast. But her gentleman friend said that he
had had his first breakfast to, but it was time for his second. So
he took Dorothy to the Half Brow house where everybody eats
white sausages and pretzels and beer at 11 oclock. So after they
had their white sausages and beer he wanted to take her for a
ride but they could only go a few blocks because by then it was
time for luncheon. So they ate quite a lot of luncheon and then
he bought her a large size box of chocolates that were full of
liqueurs, and took her to the matinee. So after the first act
Rudolf got hungry and they had to go and stand in the lobby
and have some sandwitches and beer. But Dorothy did not
enjoy the show very much and so after the second act Rudolf

said they would leave because it was time for tea anyway. So after quite a heavy tea, Rudolf asked her to dinner and Dorothy was to overcome to say No. So after dinner they went to a beer garden for beer and pretzels. But finally Dorothy began to come to, and she asked him to take her back to the hotel. So Rudolf said he would, but they had better have a bite to eat first. So today Dorothy really feels just as discouradged as I seem to feel, only Dorothy is not a Christian science and all she can do is suffer.

But in spite of all my Christian science, I am really beginning to feel quite discouradged about Vienna. I mean Mr Eisman is in Vienna, and I do not seè how I can spend quite a lot of time with Mr Eisman and quite a lot of time with Mr Spoffard and keep them from meeting one another. Because Mr Spoffard might not seem to understand why Mr Eisman seems to spend quite a lot of money to get me educated. And Dorothy keeps trying to depress me about Miss Chapman because she says she thinks that when Miss Chapman sees I and Mr Spoffard together she thinks that Miss Chapman will cable for the familys favorite lunacy expert. So I have got to be as full of Christian science as I can and always hope for the best.

May 25th

So far everything has really worked out for the best. Because
Mr Eisman is very very busy all day with the button profession, and he tells me to run around with Dorothy all day. So I
and Mr Spoffard run around all day. So then I tell Mr Spoffard
that I really do not care to go to all of the places that you go to at
night, but I will go to bed and get ready for tomorrow instead.
So then Dorothy and I go to dinner with Mr Eisman and then
we go to a show, and we stay up quite late at a cabaret called
The Chapeau Rouge and I am able to keep it all up with the aid
of champagne. So if we keep our eye out for Mr Spoffard and
do not all bump into one another when he is out looking at
things that we Americans really should not look at, it will all
work out for the best. I mean I have even stopped Mr Spoffard
looking at museums because I tell him that I like nature better,
and when you look at nature you look at it in a horse and buggy
in the park and it is much easier on the feet. So now he is
beginning to talk about how he would like me to meet his
mother, so everything really seems for the best after all.

But I have quite a hard time with Mr Eisman at night. I mean
at night Mr Eisman is in quite a state, because every time he
makes an engagement about the button factory, it is time for all
the gentlemen in Vienna to go to the coffee house and sit. Or else

every time he makes an engagement about the button factory, some Viennese gentleman gets the idea to have a picknick and they all put on short pants and bare knees and they all put a feather in their hat, and they all walk to the Tyrol. So it really discouradges Mr Eisman quite a lot. But if anyone ought to get discouradged I think that I ought to get discouradged because after all when a girl has had no sleep for a week a girl can not help it if she seems to get discouradged.

May 27th

Well finally I broke down and Mr Spoffard said that he thought a little girl like I, who was trying to reform the whole world was trying to do to much, especially beginning on a girl like Dorothy. So he said there was a famous doctor in Vienna called Dr Froyd who could stop all of my worrying because he does not give a girl medicine but he talks you out of it by psychoanalysis. So yesterday he took me to Dr Froyd. So Dr Froyd and I had quite a long talk in the english landguage. So it seems that everybody seems to have a thing called inhibitions, which is when you want to do a thing and you do not do it. So then you dream about it instead. So Dr Froyd asked me, what I seemed to dream about. So I told him that I never really dream about anything. I mean I use my brains so much in the day time that at night they do not seem to do anything else but rest. So Dr Froyd was very very surprized at a girl who did not dream about anything. So then he asked me all about my life. I mean he is very very sympathetic, and he seems to know how to draw a girl out quite a lot. I mean I told him things that I really would not even put in my diary. So then he seemed very very intreeged at a girl who always seemed to do everything she wanted to do. So he asked me if I really never wanted to do a thing that I did not do. For instance did I ever want to do a thing that was really vialent, for instance, did I ever want to shoot someone for instance. So then I said I had, but the bullet only went in Mr Jennings lung and came right out again. So then Dr Froyd looked at me and looked at me and he said he did not really think it was possible. So then he called in his assistance and he pointed at me and talked to his assistance quite a lot in the Viennese landguage. So then his assistance looked at me and looked at me and it really seems as if I was quite a famous case. So then Dr Froyd said that all I needed was to cultivate a few inhibitions and get some sleep.

May 29th

Things are really getting to be quite a strain. Because yesterday Mr Spoffard and Mr Eisman were both in the lobby of the Bristol hotel and I had to pretend not to see both of them. I mean it is quite an easy thing to pretend not to see one gentleman, but it is quite a hard thing to pretend not to see two gentlemen. So something has really got to happen soon, or I will have to admit that things seem to be happening that are not for the best.

So this afternoon Dorothy and I had an engagement to meet Count Salm for tea at four o'clock, only you do not call it tea at Vienna but you seem to call it 'yowzer' and you do not drink tea at Vienna but you drink coffee instead. I mean it is quite unusual to see all of the gentlemen at Vienna stop work, to go to yowzer about one hour after they have all finished their luncheon, but time really does not seem to mean so much to Viennese gentlemen except time to get to the coffee house, which they all seem to know by instincts, or else they really do not seem to mind if they make a mistake and get there to early. Because Mr Eisman says that when it is time to attend to the button profession, they really seem to lose all of their interest until Mr Eisman is getting so nervous he could scream.

So we went to Deimels and met Count Salm. But while we

were having yowzer with Count Salm, we saw Mr Spoffard's mother come in with her companion Miss Chapman, and Miss Chapman seemed to look at me quite a lot and talk to Mr Spoffards mother about me quite a lot. So I became quite nervous, because I really wished that we were not with Count Salm. I mean it has been quite a hard thing to make Mr Spoffard think that I am trying to reform Dorothy, but if I had to try to make him think that I was trying to reform Count Salm, he might begin to think that there is a limit to almost everything. So Mr Spoffards mother seems to be deaf, because she seems to use an ear trumpet and I really could not help over hearing quite a lot of words that Miss Chapman was using on me, even if it is not such good etiquet to overhear people. So Miss Chapman seemed to be telling Mr Spoffards mother that I was a 'creature', and she seemed to be telling her that I was the real reason why her son seemed to be so full of nothing but neglect lately. So then Mr Spoffards mother looked at me and looked at me, even if it was not such good etiquet to look at a person. And Miss Chapman kept right on talking to Mr Spoffards mother and I heard her mention Willie Gwynn and I think that Miss Chapman has been making some inquiries about me and I really think that she has heard about the time when all of the family of Willie Gwynn had quite a long talk with me and persuaded me not to marry Willie Gwynn for $10,000. So I really wish Mr Spoffard would introduce me to his mother before she gets to be full of quite a lot of prejudice. Because one thing seems to be piling up on top of another thing, until I am almost on the verge of getting nervous and I have not had any time yet to do what Dr Froyd said a girl ought to do.

So tonight I am going to tell Mr Eisman that I have got to go to bed early, so then I can take quite a long ride with Mr Spoffard and look at nature, and he may say something definite, because nothing makes gentlemen get so definite as looking at nature when it is moonlight.

May 30th

Well last night Mr Spoffard and I took quite a long ride in the park, but they do not call it a park in the Viennese landguage but they call it the Prater. So a prater is really devine because it is just like Coney Island but at the same time it is in the woods and it is practically full of trees and it has quite a long road for people to take rides on in a horse and buggy. So I found out that Miss Chapman has been talking against me quite a lot. So it seems that she has been making inquiries about me, and I was really surprised to hear all of the things that Miss Chapman seemed to find out about me except that she did not find out about Mr Eisman educating me. So then I had to tell Mr Spoffard that I was not always so reformed as I am now, because the world was full of gentlemen who were nothing but wolfs in sheeps clothes, that did nothing but take advantadge of all we girls. So I really cried quite a lot. So then I told him how I was just a little girl from Little Rock when I first left Little Rock and by that time even Mr Spoffard had tears in his eyes. So I told him how I came from a very very good family because papa was very intelectual, and he was a very very prominent Elk, and everybody always said that he was a very intelectual Elk. So I told Mr Spoffard that when I left Little Rock I thought that all of the gentlemen did not want to do anything but protect we girls and by the time I found out that they did not want to protect us so much, it was to late. So then he cried quite a lot. So then I told him how I finaly got reformed by reading all about him in the newspapers and when I saw him in the oriental express it really seemed to be nothing but the result of fate. So I told Mr Spoffard that I thought a girl was really more reformed if she knew what it was to be unreformed than if she was born reformed and never really knew what was the matter with her. So then Mr Spoffard reached over and he kissed me on the forehead in a way that was full of reverance and he said I seemed to remind him quite a lot of a girl who got quite a write-up in the bible who was called Magdellen. So then he said that he used to be a member of the choir himself, so who was he to cast the first rock at a girl like I.

So we rode around in the Prater until it was quite late and it really was devine because it was moonlight and we talked quite a lot about morals, and all the bands in the prater were all playing in the distants 'Mama love Papa'. Because 'Mama love Papa' has just reached Vienna and they all seem to be crazy about 'Mama love Papa' even if it is not so new in America. So then he took me home to the hotel.

So everything always works out for the best, because this morning Mr Spoffard called up and told me he wanted me to meet his mother. So I told him I would like to have luncheon alone with his mother because we could have quite a little tatatate if there was only two of us. So I told him to bring his mother to our room for luncheon because I thought that Miss Chapman could not walk into our room and spoil everything.

So he brought his mother down to our sitting room and I put on quite a simple little organdy gown that I had ripped all of the trimming off of, and I had a pair of black lace mitts that Dorothy used to wear in the Follies and I had a pair of shoes that did not have any heels on them. So when he introduced us to each other I dropped her a courtesy because I always think it is quite quaint when a girl drops quite a lot of courtesys. So then he left us alone and we had quite a little talk and I told her that I did not seem to like all of the flappers that we seem to have nowadays, because I was brought up to be more old fashioned.

So then Mr Spoffards mother told me that Miss Chapman said that she had heard that I was not so old fashioned. But I told her that I was so old fashioned that I was always full of respect for all of my elders and I would not dare to tell them everything they ought to do, like Miss Chapman seems to tell her everything she ought to do, for instants.

So then I ordered luncheon and I thought some champagne would make her feel quite good for luncheon so I asked her if she liked champagne. So she really likes champagne very very much but Miss Chapman thinks it is not so nice for a person to drink liquor. But I told her that I was a Christian science, and all of we Christian science seem to believe that there can not really be any harm in anything, so how can there be any harm in a small size bottle of champagne? So she never seemed to look at it in that kind of a light before, because she said that Miss Chapman believed in Christian science also, but what Miss Chapman believed about things that were good for you to drink seemed to apply more towards water. So then we had luncheon and she began to feel very very good. So I thought that we had better have another bottle of champagne because I told her that I was such an ardent Christian science that I did not even believe there could be any harm in two bottles of champagne. So we had another bottle of champagne and she became very intreeged about Christian science because she said that she really thought it was a better religion than Prespyterians. So she said Miss Chapman used to try to get her to use it on things, but Miss Chapman never seemed to have such a large size grasp of the Christian science religion as I seem to have.

So then I told her that I thought Miss Chapman was jealous of her good looks. So then she said that that was true, because Miss Chapman would always make her wear hats that were made out of black horses hair because horses hair does not weigh so much on a persons brain. So I told her I was going to give her one of my hats that has got quite large size roses on it. So then I got it out, but we could not get it on her head because hats are quite small on account of hair being bobbed. So I thought I would get the sissors and bob her head, but then I thought I had done enough to her for one day.

So Henry's mother said that I was really the most sunshine that she ever had in all her life and when Henry came back to take his Mother up to her room, she did not want to go. But after he got her away he called me up on the telephone and he was quite excited and he said he wanted to ask me something that was very important. So I said I would see him tonight.

But now I have got to see Mr Eisman because I have an idea about doing something that is really very very important that has got to be done at once.

May 31st

Well I and Dorothy and Mr Eisman are on a train going to a place called Buda Pest. So I did not see Henry again before I left, but I left him a letter. Because I thought it would be a quite good thing if what he wanted to ask me he would have to write down, instead of asking me, and he could not write it to me if I was in the same city that he is in. So I told him in my letter that I had to leave in five minute's time because I found out that Dorothy was just on the verge of getting very unreformed, and if I did not get her away, all I had done for her would really go for nothing. So I told him to write down what he had to say to me, and mail it to me at the Ritz hotel in Buda Pest. Because I always seem to believe in the old addage, Say it in writing.

So it was really very easy to get Mr Eisman to leave Vienna, because yesterday he went out to see the button factory but it seems that all of the people at the button factory were not at work but they were giving a birthday party to some saint. So it seems that every time some saint has a birthday they all stop work so they can give it a birthday party. So Mr Eisman looked at their calendar, and found out that some saint or other was born practically every week in the year. So he has decided that America is good enough for him.

So Henry will not be able to follow me to Buda Pest because

his mother is having treatments by Dr Froyd and she seems to be a much more difficult case than I seem to be. I mean it is quite hard for Dr Froyd, because she cannot seem to remember which is a dream and which really happened to her. So she tells him everything, and he has to use his judgement. I mean when she tells him that a very very handsome young gentleman tried to flirt with her on Fifth Avenue, he uses his judgement.

So we will soon be at a Ritz hotel again and I must say it will be delightful to find a Ritz hotel right in the central of Europe.

June 1st

Well yesterday Henrys letter came and it says in black and white that he and his mother have never met such a girl as I and he wants me to marry him. So I took Henrys letter to the photographers and I had quite a lot of photographs taken of it because a girl might lose Henrys letter and she would not have anything left to remember him by. But Dorothy says to hang on to Henry's letter, because she really does not think the photographs do it justice.

So this afternoon I got a telegram from Henry and the telegram says that Henry's father is very, very ill in New York and they have got to leave for New York immediately and his heart is broken not to see me again and to send him my answer by telegraph so that his mind will be rested while he is going back to New York. So I sent him a telegram and I accepted his proposal. So tonight I got another telegram and Henry says that he and his mother are very very happy and Henrys mother can hardly bear Miss Chapman any more and Henry says he hopes I will decide to come right back to New York and keep his mother quite a lot of company, because he thinks I can reform Dorothy more in New York anyway, where there is prohibition and nobody can get anything to drink.

So now I have got to make up my mind whether I really want

to marry Henry after all. Because I know to much to get married to any gentleman like Henry without thinking it all over. Because Henry is the kind of a gentleman who gets on a girls nerves quite a lot and when a gentleman has nothing else to do but get on a girls nerves, there really seems to be a limit to almost everything. Because when a gentleman has a business, he has an office and he has to be there, but when a gentlemans business is only looking into other peoples business, a gentleman is always on the verge of coming in and out of the house. And a girl could not really say that her time was her own. And when Henry was not in and out of the house, his mother would always be in and out of the house because she seems to think that I am so full of nothing but sunshine. So it is quite a problem and I seem to be in quite a quarandary, because it might really be better if Henry should happen to decide that he should not get married, and he should change his mind, and desert a girl, and then it would only be right if a girl should sue him for a breach of promise.

But I really think, whatever happens, that Dorothy and I had better get back to New York. So I will see if Mr Eisman will send us back. I mean I really do not think that Mr Eisman will mind us going back because if he does, I will start shopping again and that always seems to bring him to terms. But all the time I am going back to New York, I will have to try to make up my mind one way or another. Because we girls really can not help it, if we have ideals, and sometimes my mind seems to get to running on things that are romantic, and I seem to think that maybe there is some place in the world where there is a gentleman who knows how to look and act like Count Salm and who has got money besides. And when a girls mind gets to thinking about such a romantic thing, a girls mind really does not seem to know whether to marry Henry or not.

Brains Are Really Everything

Chapter Six

June 14th

Well, Dorothy and I arrived at New York yesterday because Mr Eisman finally decided to send us home because he said that all of his button profession would not stand the strain of educating me much more in Europe. So we separated from Mr Eisman in Buda Pest because Mr Eisman had to go to Berlin to look up all his starving relatives in Berlin, who have done nothing but starve since the War, so he wrote me just before we sailed and he said that he had dug up all his starving relatives and he had looked them all over, and decided not to bring them to America because there was not one of his starving relatives who could travel on a railroad ticket without paying excess fare for overweight.

So Dorothy and I took the boat and all the way over on the boat I had to make up my mind whether I really wanted to marry the famous Henry H. Spoffard, or not, because he was waiting for me to arrive at New York and he was so impatient that he could hardly wait for me to arrive at New York. But I have not wasted all of my time on Henry, even if I do not marry him, because I have some letters from Henry which would come in very, very handy if I did not marry Henry. So Dorothy seems to agree with me quite a lot, because Dorothy says the only thing she could stand being to Henry, would be to be his widow at the age of 18.

So coming over on the boat I decided not to bother to meet any gentlemen, because what good does it do to meet gentlemen when there is nothing to do on a boat but go shopping at a little shop where they do not have any thing that costs more than five dollars. And besides if I did meet any gentleman on the boat, he would want to see me off the boat, and then we would bump into Henry. But then I heard that there was a gentleman on the boat who was quite a dealer in unset diamonds from a town called Amsterdam. So I met the gentleman, and we went around together quite a lot, but we had quite a quarrel the night before we landed, so I did not even bother to look at him when I came down the gangplank, and I put the unset diamonds in my handbag so I did not have to declare them at the customs.

So Henry was waiting for me at the customs, because he had come up from Pennsylvania to meet me, because their country estate is at Pennsylvania, and Henry's father is very, very ill at Pennsylvania, so Henry has to stay there practically all of the time. So all of the reporters were at the customs and they all heard about how Henry and I were engaged to one another and they wanted to know what I was before I became engaged to Henry, so I told them that I was nothing but a society girl from Little Rock, Arkansas. So then I became quite angry with Dorothy because one of the reporters asked Dorothy when I made my debut in society at Little Rock and Dorothy said I made my debut at the Elks annual street fair and carnival at the age of 15. I mean Dorothy never overlooks any chance to be unrefined, even when she is talking to literary gentlemen like reporters.

So Henry brought me to the apartment in his Rolls Royce, and while we were coming to the apartment he said he wanted to give me my engagement ring and I really became all thrills. So he said that he had gone to Cartiers and he had looked over all the engagement rings in Cartiers and after he had looked them all over he had decided that they were not half good enough for me. So then he took a box out of his pocket and I really became intreeged. So then Henry said that when he looked at all of those large size diamonds he really felt that they did not have any sentiment, so he was going to give me his class ring from Amherst College insted. So then I looked at him and looked at him, but I am to full of self controle to say anything at this stage of the game, so I said it was really very sweet of him to be so full of nothing but sentiment.

So then Henry said that he would have to go back to Pennsylvania to talk to his father about us getting married, because his father has really got his heart set on us not getting married. So I told Henry that perhaps if I would meet his father, I would win him over, because I always seem to win gentlemen over. But Henry says that that is just the trouble, because some girl is always winning his father over, and they hardly dare to let him go out of their sight, and they hardly dare let him go to church alone. Because the last time he went to church alone some girl won him over on the street corner and he arrived back home with all of his pocket money gone, and they could not believe him when he said that he had put it in the plate, because he has not put more than a dime in the plate for the last fifty years.

So it seems that the real reason why his father does not want Henry to marry me, is because his father says that Henry always has all of the fun, and every time Henry's father wants to have some fun of his own, Henry always stops him and Henry will not even let him be sick at a hospital where he could have some fun of his own, but he keeps him at home where he has to have a nurse Henry picked out for him who is a male nurse. So all of his objections seem to be nothing but the spirit of resiprosity. But Henry says that all his objections cannot last much longer because he is nearly 90 years of age after all, and Nature must take its course sooner or later.

So Dorothy says what a fool I am to waste my time on Henry, when I might manage to meet Henry's father and the whole thing would be over in a few months and I would practically own the state of Pennsylvania. But I do not think I ought to take Dorothy's advise because Henry's father is watched like a hawk and Henry himself is his Power of Attorney, so no good could really come of it after all. And, after all, why should I listen to the advise of a girl like Dorothy who traveled all over Europe and all she came home with was a bangle!

So Henry spent the evening at the apartment and then he had to go back to Pennsylvania to be there Thursday morning, because every Thursday morning he belongs to a society who do nothing but senshure all of the photoplays. So they cut out all of the pieces out of all the photoplays that show things that are riskay, that people ought not to look at. So then they put all of the riskay pieces together and they run them over and over again. So it would really be quite a hard thing to drag Henry away from one of his Thursday mornings and he can hardly wait from one Thursday morning to another. Because he really does not seem to enjoy anything so much as senshuring photoplays and after a photoplay has once been senshured he seems to lose all of his interest in it.

So after Henry left I held quite a conversation with Lulu, who is my maid who looked out for my apartment while I was away. So Lulu really thinks I ought to marry Mr Spoffard after all, because Lulu says that she kept studying Mr Spoffard all of the time she was unpacking my trunks, and Lulu says she is sure that any time I feel as if I had to get away from Mr Spoffard I could just set him down on the floor, and give him a packet of riskay french postcards to senshure and stay away as long as I like.

So Henry is going to arrange for me to come down to Pennsylvania for a week-end and meet all of his family. But if all of Henry's family are as full of reforms as Henry seems to be, it will be quite an ordeal even for a girl like I.

June 15th

Yesterday morning was quite an ordeal for a refined girl because all of the newspapers all printed the story of how Henry and I are engaged to one another, but they all seemed to leave out the part about me being a society girl except one newspaper, and that was the newspaper that quoted what Dorothy said about me being a debutant at the Elk's Carnival. So I called up Dorothy at the Ritz and I told Dorothy that a girl like she ought to keep her mouth closed in the presents of reporters.

So it seems that quite a lot of reporters kept calling Dorothy up but Dorothy said she really did not say anything to any of them except one reporter asked her what I used for money and she told him buttons. But Dorothy really should not have said such a thing, because quite a few people seem to know that Mr Eisman is educating me and that he is known all over Chicago as Gus Eisman the Button King, so one thing might suggest another until people's minds might begin to think something.

But Dorothy said that she did not say anything more about me being a debutant at Little Rock, because after all Dorothy knows that I really did not make any debut in Little Rock, because just when it was time to make my debut, my gentleman friend Mr Jennings became shot, and after the trial was over and all of the Jury had let me off, I was really much to fatigued to make my debut.

So then Dorothy said, why don't we throw a party now and you can become a debutant now and put them all in their place, because it seems that Dorothy is dying for a party. So that is really the first sensible suggestion that Dorothy has made yet, because I think that every girl who is engaged to a gentleman who has a fine old family like Henry, had really ought to be a debutant. So I told her to come right over and we would plan my debut but we would keep it very, very quiet and give it tomorrow night, because if Henry heard I was making my debut he would come up from Pennsylvania and he would practically spoil the party, because all Henry has to do to spoil a party is to arrive at it.

So Dorothy came over and we planned my debut. So first we decided to have some engraved invitations engraved, but it always takes quite a little time to have invitations engraved, and it would really be foolish because all of the gentlemen we were going to invite to my debut were all members of the Racquet Club, so I could just write out a notice that I was having a debut and give it to Willie Gwynn and have Willie Gwynn post it on the Racquet Club board.

So Willie Gwynn posted it on the club board and then he called me up and he told me that he had never seen so much enthusiasm since the Dempsey-Firpo fight, and he said that the whole Racquet Club would be there in a body. So then we had to plan about what girls we would ask to my debut. Because I have not seemed to meet so many society women yet because of course a girl does not meet society women until her debut is all over, and then all the society women all come and call on a debutant. But I know practically all of the society men, because practically all of the society men belong to the Racquet club, so after I have the Racquet Club at my debut, all I have to do to take my real place in society is to meet their mothers and sisters, because I know practically all of their sweethearts now.

But I always seem to think that it is delightful to have quite a lot of girls at a party, if a girl has quite a lot of gentlemen at a party, and it is quite delightful to have all the girls from the

Follies, but I really could not invite them because, after all, they are not in my set. So then I thought it all over and I thought that even if it was not etiquette to invite them to a party, it really would be etiquette to hire them to come to a party and be entertainers, and after they were entertainers they could mix in to the party and it really would not be a social error.

So then the telephone rang and Dorothy answered it and it seems that it was Joe Sanguinetti, who is almost the official bootlegger for the whole Racquet Club, and Joe said he had heard about my debut and if he could come to my debut and bring his club which is the Silver Spray Social Club of Brooklyn, he would supply all of the liquor and he would guarantee to practically run the rum fleet up to the front door.

So Dorothy told him he could come, and she hung up the telephone before she told me his proposition, and I became quite angry with Dorothy because, after all, the Silver Spray Social Club is not even mentioned in the Social Register and it has no place at a girl's debut. But Dorothy said by the time the party got into swing, anyone would have to be a genius if he could tell whether he belonged to the Racquet Club, the Silver Spray Social Club, or the Knights of Pythias. But I really was almost sorry that I asked Dorothy to help plan my debut, except that Dorothy is very good to have at a party if the police come in, because Dorothy always knows how to manage the police, and I never knew a policeman yet who did not finish up by being madly in love with Dorothy. So then Dorothy called up all of the reporters on all of the newspapers and invited them all to my debut, so they could see it with their own eyes.

So Dorothy says that she is going to see to it that my debut lands on the front page of all of the newspapers, if we have to commit a murder to do it.

June 19th

Well, it has been three days since my debut party started but I finally got tired and left the party last night and went to bed because I always seem to lose all of my interest in a party after a few days, but Dorothy never loses her interest in a party and when I woke up this morning Dorothy was just saying goodbye to some of the guests. I mean Dorothy seems to have quite a lot of vitality, because the last guests of the party were guests we picked up when the party went to take a swim at Long Beach the day before yesterday, and they were practically fresh, but Dorothy had gone clear through the party from beginning to end without even stopping to go to a Turkish bath as most of the gentlemen had to do. So my debut has really been very novel, because quite a lot of the guests who finished up at my debut were not the same guests that started out at it, and it is really quite novel for a girl to have so many different kinds of gentlemen at her debut. So it has really been a very great success because all of the newspapers have quite a lot of write-ups about my debut and I really felt quite proud when I saw the front page of the *Daily Views* and it said in large size headlines, 'LORELEI'S DEBUT A WOW!' And *Zits' Weekly* came right out and said that if this party marks my entrance into society, they only hope that they can live to see what I will spring once I have overcome my debutant reserve and taken my place in the world.

So I really had to apologize to Dorothy about asking Joe Sanguinetti to my debut because it was wonderful the way he got all of the liquor to the party and he more than kept his word. I mean he had his bootleggers run up from the wharf in taxis, right to the apartment, and the only trouble he had was, that once the bootleggers delivered the liquor, he could not get them to leave the party. So finally there was quite a little quarrel because Willie Gwynn claimed that Joe's bootleggers were snubbing the members of his club because they would not let the boys from the Racquet club sing in their quartet. But Joe's bootleggers said that the Racquet club boys wanted to sing songs that were unrefined, while they wanted to sing songs about Mother. So then everybody started to take sides, but the girls from the Follies were all with Joe's bootleggers from the start because practically all we girls were listening to them with tears steaming from our eyes. So that made the Racquet club jealous and one thing led to another until somebody rang for an ambulants and then the police came in.

So Dorothy, as usual, won over all of the police. So it seems that the police all have orders from Judge Schultzmeyer, who is the famous judge who tries all of the prohibition cases, that any time they break into a party that looks like it was going to be a good party, to call him up no matter what time of the day or night it is, because Judge Schultzmeyer dearly loves a party. So the Police called up Judge Schultzmeyer and he was down in less than no time. So during the party both Joe Sanguinetti and Judge Schultzmeyer fell madly in love with Dorothy. So Joe and the Judge had quite a little quarrel and the Judge told Joe that if his stuff was fit to drink he would set the Law after him and confiscate it, but his stuff was not worth the while of any gentleman to confiscate who had any respect for his stomach, and he would not lower himself to confiscate it. So along about nine o'clock in the morning Judge Schultzmeyer had to leave the party and go to court to try all of the criminals who break all of the laws, so he had to leave Dorothy and Joe together and he was very very angry. And I really felt quite sorry for any person who went up before Judge Schultzmeyer that morning, because he gave everybody 90 days and was back at the party by twelve o'clock. So then he stuck to the party until we were all going down to Long Beach to take a swim day before yesterday when he seemed to become unconscious, so we dropped him off at a sanitorium in Garden City.

So my debut party was really the greatest success of the social season, because the second night of my debut party was the night when Willie Gwynn's sister was having a dance at the Gwynn estate on Long Island, and Willie Gwynn said that all of the eligible gentlemen in New York were conspicuous by their absents at his sister's party, because they were all at my party. So it seems as if I am really going to be quite a famous hostess if I can just bring my mind to the point of being Mrs Henry Spoffard Jr.

Well Henry called up this morning and Henry said he had finally got his father's mind so that he thought it was safe for me to meet him and he was coming up to get me this afternoon so that I can meet his family and see his famous old historical home at Pennsylvania. So then he asked about my debut party which some of the Philadelphia papers seemed to mention. But I told him that my debut was really not so much planned, as it was spontaneous, and I did not have the heart to call him up at a moments notice and take him away from his father at such a time for reasons which were nothing but social.

So now I am getting ready to visit Henry's family and I feel as if my whole future depends on it. Because if I can not stand Henry's family any more than I can stand Henry the whole thing will probly come to an end in the law court.

June 21st

Well, I am now spending the weekend with Henry's family at his old family mansion outside of Philadelphia, and I am beginning to think, after all, that there is something else in the world besides family. And I am beginning to think that family life is only fit for those who can stand it. For instants, they always seem to get up very early in Henry's family. I mean it really is not so bad to get up early when there is something to get up early about, but when a girl gets up early and there is nothing to get up early about, it really begins to seem as if there was no sense to it.

So yesterday we all got up early and that was when I met all of Henry's family, because Henry and I motored down to Pennsylvania and everybody was in bed when we arrived because it was after nine o'clock. So in the morning Henry's mother came to my room to get me up in time for breakfast because Henry's mother is very very fond of me, and she always wants to copy all of my gowns and she always loves to look through all of my things to see what I have got. So she found a box of liqueur candies that are full of liqueurs and she was really very delighted. So I finally got dressed and she threw the empty box away and I helped her down stairs to the Dining room.

So Henry was waiting in the dining room with his sister and

that was when I met his sister. So it seems that Henry's sister has never been the same since the war, because she never had on a man's collar and a necktie until she drove an ambulants in the war, and now they cannot get her to take them off. Because ever since the armistice Henry's sister seems to have the idea that regular womens clothes are effiminate. So Henry's sister seems to think of nothing but either horses or automobiles and when she is not in a garage the only other place she is happy in is a stable. I mean she really pays very little attention to all of her family and she seems to pay less attention to Henry than anybody else because she seems to have the idea that Henry's brains are not so viril. So then we all waited for Henry's father to come in so that he could read the Bible out loud before breakfast.

So then something happened that really was a miracle. Because it seems that Henry's father has practically lived in a wheel chair for months and months and his male nurse has to wheel him everywhere. So his male nurse wheeled him into the dining room in his wheel chair and then Henry said 'Father, this is going to be your little daughter in law,' and Henry's father took one good look at me and got right out of his wheel chair and walked! So then everybody was very very surprised, but Henry was not so surprised because Henry knows his father like a book. So then they all tried to calm his father down, and his father tried to read out of the Bible but he could hardly keep his mind on the Bible and he could hardly eat a bite because when a gentleman is as feeble as Henry's father is, he cannot keep one eye on a girl and the other eye on his cereal and cream without coming to grief. So Henry finally became quite discouradged and he told his father he would have to get back to his room or he would have a relapse. So then the male nurse wheeled him back to his room and it really was pathetic because he cried like a baby. So I got to thinking over what Dorothy advised me about Henry's father and I really got to thinking that if Henry's father could only get away from everybody and have some time of his own, Dorothy's advise might not be so bad after all.

So after breakfast we all got ready to go to church, but Henry's sister does not go to church because Henry's sister always likes to spend every Sunday in the garage taking their

Ford farm truck apart and putting it back together again, and Henry says that what the war did to a girl like his sister is really worse than the war itself.

So then Henry and his mother and I all went to church. So we came home from church and we had luncheon and it seems that luncheon is practically the same as breakfast except that Henry's father could not come down to luncheon because after he met me he contracted such a vialent fever that they had to send for the Doctor.

So in the afternoon Henry went to prayer meeting and I was left alone with Henry's mother so that we could rest up so that we could go to church again after supper. So Henry's mother thinks I am nothing but sunshine and she will hardly let me get out of her sight, because she hates to be by herself because, when she is by herself, her brains hardly seem to work at all. So she loves to try on all of my hats and she loves to tell me how all the boys in the choir can hardly keep their eyes off her. So of course a girl has to agree with her, and it is quite difficult to agree with a person when you have to do it through an ear trumpet because sooner or later your voice has to give out.

So then supper turned out to be practically the same thing as luncheon only by supper time all of the novelty seemed to wear off. So then I told Henry that I had to much of a headache to go to church again, so Henry and his mother went to church and I went to my room and I sat down and thought and I decided that life was really to short to spend it in being proud of your family, even if they did have a great deal of money. So the best thing for me to do is to think up some scheme to make Henry decide not to marry me and take what I can get out of it and be satisfied.

June 22nd

Well, yesterday I made Henry put me on the train at Philadelphia and I made him stay at Philadelphia so he could be near his father if his father seemed to take any more relapses. So I sat in my drawing room on the train and I decided that the time had come to get rid of Henry at any cost. So I decided that the thing that discouradges gentlemen more than anything else is shopping. Because even Mr Eisman, who was practically born for we girls to shop on, and who knows just what to expect, often gets quite discouradged over all of my shopping. So I decided I would get to New York and I would go to Cartiers and run up quite a large size bill on Henry's credit, because after all our engagement has been announced in all of the newspapers, and Henry's credit is really my credit.

So while I was thinking it all over there was a knock on the drawing room door, so I told him to come in and it was a gentleman who said he had seen me quite a lot in New York and he had always wanted to have an introduction to me, because we had quite a lot of friends who were common. So then he gave me his card and his name was on his card and it was Mr Gilbertson Montrose and his profession is a senario writer. So then I asked him to sit down and we held a literary conversation.

So I really feel as if yesterday was a turning point in my life, because at last I have met a gentleman who is not only an artist but who has got brains besides. I mean he is the kind of gentleman that a girl could sit at his feet and listen to for days and days and nearly always learn something or other. Because, after all, there is nothing that gives a girl more of a thrill than brains in a gentleman, especially after a girl has been spending the week end with Henry. So Mr Montrose talked and talked all of the way to New York and I sat there and did nothing else but listen. So according to Mr Montrose's opinion Shakespear is a very great playwrite, and he thinks that Hamlet is quite a famous tragedy and as far as novels are concerned he believes that nearly everybody had ought to read Dickens. And when we got on the subject of poetry he recited 'The Shooting of Dan McGrew' until you could almost hear the gun go off.

And then I asked Mr Montrose to tell me all about himself. So it seems that Mr Montrose was on his way home from Washington DC, where he went to see the Bulgarian Ambassadore to see if he could get Bulgaria to finance a senario he has written which is a great historical subject which is founded on the sex life of Dolly Madison. So it seems that Mr Montrose has met quite a lot of Bulgarians in a Bulgarian restaurant on Lexington Avenue and that was what gave him the idea to get the money from Bulgaria. Because Mr Montrose said that he could fill his senario full of Bulgarian propaganda, and he told the Bulgarian Ambassadore that every time he realized how ignorant all of the American film fans were on the subject of Bulgaria, it made him flinch.

So I told Mr Montrose that it made me feel very very small to talk to a gentleman like he, who knew so much about Bulgaria, because practically all I knew about Bulgaria was Zoolack. So Mr Montrose said that the Bulgarian Ambassadore did not seem to think that Dolly Madison had so much about her that was pertinent to present day Bulgaria, but Mr Montrose explained to him that that was because he knew practically nothing about dramatic construction. Because Mr Montrose said he could fix his senario so that Dolly Madison would have one lover who was a Bulgarian, who wanted to marry her. So then Dolly Madison would get to wondering what her great,

great grandchildren would be like if she married a Bulgarian, and then she could sit down and have a vision of Bulgaria in 1925. So that was when Mr Montrose would take a trip to Bulgaria to photograph the vision. But the Bulgarian Ambassadore turned down the whole proposition, but he gave Mr Montrose quite a large size bottle of the Bulgarian national drink. So the Bulgarian national drink looks like nothing so much as water, and it really does not taste so strong, but about five minutes afterwards you begin to realize your mistake. But I thought to myself that if realizing my mistake could make me forget what I went through in Pennsylvania, I really owed it to myself to forget everything. So then we had another drink.

So then Mr Montrose told me that he had quite a hard time getting along in the motion picture profession, because all of his senarios are all over their head. Because when Mr Montrose writes about sex, it is full of sychology, but when everybody else writes about it, it is full of nothing but transparent negligays and ornamental bath tubs. And Mr Montrose says that there is no future in the motion pictures until the motion pictures get their sex motives straightened out, and realize that a woman of 25 can have just as many sex problems as a flapper of 16. Because Mr Montrose likes to write about women of the world, and he refuses to have women of the world played by small size girls of 15 who know nothing about life and who have not even been in the detention home.

So we both arrived in New York before we realized it, and I got to thinking how the same trip with Henry in his Rolls Royce seemed like about 24 hours, and that was what gave me the idea that money was not everything, because after all, it is only brains that count. So Mr Montrose took me home and we are going to have luncheon together at the Primrose Tea room practically every day and keep right on holding literary conversations.

So then I had to figure out how to get rid of Henry and at the same time not do anything that would make me any trouble later. So I sent for Dorothy because Dorothy is not so good at intreeging a gentleman with money, but she ought to be full of ideas on how to get rid of one.

So at first Dorothy said, Why didn't I take a chance and marry Henry because she had an idea that if Henry married me he would commit suicide about two weeks later. But I told her about my plan to do quite a lot of shopping, and I told her that I would send for Henry and I would manage it so that I would not be in the apartment when he came, but she could be there and start a conversation with him and she could tell him about all of my shopping and how extravagant I seemed to be and he would be in the poor house in less than a year if he married me.

So Dorothy said for me to take one farewell look at Henry and leave him to her, because the next time I saw him would be in the witness box and I might not even recognize him because she would throw a scare into him that might change his whole physical appearance. So I decided to leave him in the hands of Dorothy and hope for the best.

July 10th

Well, last month was really almost a diary in itself, and I have to begin to realize that I am one of the kind of girls that things happen to. And I have to admit, after all, that life is really wonderful. Because so much has happened in the last few weeks that it almost makes a girl's brains whirl.

I mean in the first place I went shopping at Cartiers and bought quite a delightful square cut emerald and quite a long rope of pearls on Henry's credit. So then I called up Henry on the long distants telephone and told him that I wanted to see him quite a lot, so he was very very pleased and he said that he would come right up to New York.

So then I told Dorothy to come to the apartment and be there when Henry came, and to show Henry what I bought on his credit, and to tell him how extravagant I seem to be, and how I seem to keep on getting worse. So I told Dorothy to go as far as she liked, so long as she did not insinuate anything against my character, because the more spotless my character seems to be, the better things might turn out later. So Henry was due at the apartment about 1.20, so I had Lulu get some luncheon for he and Dorothy and I told Dorothy to tell him that I had gone out to look at the Russian Crown Jewels that some Russian Grand Duchess or other had for sale at the Ritz.

So then I went to the Primrose Tea Room to have luncheon with Mr Montrose because Mr Montrose loves to tell me of all his plans, and he says that I seem to remind him quite a lot of a girl called Madame Recamier who all the intelectual gentlemen used to tell all of their plans to, even when there was a French revolution going on all around them.

So Mr Montrose and I had a delicious luncheon, except that I never seem to notice what I am eating when I am with Mr Montrose because when Mr Montrose talks a girl wants to do nothing but listen. But all of the time I was listening, I was thinking about Dorothy and I was worrying for fear Dorothy would go to far, and tell Henry something that would not be so good for me afterwards. So finally even Mr Montrose seemed to notice it, and he said, 'What's the matter little woman, a penny for your thoughts.'

So then I told him everything. So he seemed to think quite a lot and finally he said to me 'It is really to bad that you feel as if the social life of Mr Spoffard bored you, because Mr Spoffard would be ideal to finance my senario.' So then Mr Montrose said that he had been thinking from the very first how ideal I would be to play Dolly Madison. So that started me thinking and I told Mr Montrose that I expected to have quite a large size ammount of money later on, and I would finance it myself. But Mr Montrose said that would be to late, because all of the motion picture corporations were after it now, and it would be snaped up almost immediately.

So then I became almost in a panick, because I suddenly decided that if I married Henry and worked in the motion pictures at the same time, society life with Henry would not really be so bad. Because if a girl was so busy as all that, it really would not seem to matter so much if she had to stand Henry when she was not busy. But then I realized what Dorothy was up to, and I told Mr Montrose that I was almost afraid it was to late. So I hurried to the telephone and I called up Dorothy at the apartment and I asked her what she had said to Henry. So Dorothy said that she showed him the square cut emerald and told him that I bought it as a knick-knack to go with a green dress, but I had got a spot on the dress, so I was going to give them both to

Lulu. So she said she showed him the pearls and she said that after I had bought them, I was sorry I did not get pink ones because white ones were so common, so I was going to have Lulu unstring them and sew them on a negligay. So then she told him she was rather sorry I meant to buy the Russian Crown jewels because she had a feeling they were unlucky, but that I had said to her, that if I found out they were, I could toss them over my left shoulder into the Hudson river some night when there was a new moon, and it would take away the curse.

So then she said that Henry began to get restless. So then she told him she was very glad I was going to get married at last because I had had such bad luck, that every time I became engaged something seemed to happen to my fiance. So Henry asked her what, for instance. So Dorothy said a couple were in the insane asylum, one had shot himself for debt, and the county farm was taking care of the remainder. So Henry asked her how they got that way. So Dorothy told him it was nothing but my extravagants, and she told him that she was surprised that he had never heard about it, because all I had to do was to take luncheon at the Ritz with some prominent broker and the next day the bottom would drop out of the market. And she told him that she did not want to insinuate anything, but that I had dined with a very, very prominent German the day before German marks started to colapse.

So I became almost frantic and I told Dorothy to hold Henry at the apartment until I could get up there and explain. So I held the telephone while Dorothy went to see if Henry would wait. So Dorothy came back in a minute and she said that the parlor was empty, but that if I would hurry down to Broadway no doubt I would see a cloud of dust heading towards the Pennsylvania station, and that would be Henry.

So then I went back to Mr Montrose, and I told him that I must catch Henry at the Pennsylvania Station at any cost. And if anyone were to say that we left the Primrose tea room in a hurry, they would be putting it quite mildly. So we got to the Pennsylvania station and I just had time to get on board the train to Philadelphia and I left Mr Montrose standing at the train biting his finger nails in all of his anxiety. But I called out to him to go to his Hotel and I would telephone the result as soon as the train arrived.

So then I went through the train, and there was Henry with a look on his face which I shall never forget. So when he saw me he really seemed to shrink to $\frac{1}{2}$ his natural size. So I sat down beside him and I told him that I was really ashamed of how he acted, and if his love for me could not stand a little test that I and Dorothy had thought up, more in the spirit of fun than anything else, I never wanted to speak to such a gentleman again. And I told him that if he could not tell the difference between a real square cut emerald and one from the ten cent store, that he ought to be ashamed of himself. And I told him that if he thought that every string of white beads were pearls, it was no wonder he could make such a mistake in judging the character of a girl. So then I began to cry because of all of Henry's lack of faith. So then he tried to cheer me up but I was to hurt to even give him a decent word until we were past Newark. But by the time we were past Newark, Henry was crying himself, and it always makes me feel so tender hearted to listen to a gentleman cry that I finally forgave him. So, of course, as soon as I got home I had to take them back to Cartiers.

So then I explained to Henry how I wanted our life to mean something and I wanted to make the World a better place than it seemed to have been yet. And I told him that he knew so much about the film profession on account of senshuring all of the films that I thought he had ought to go into the film profession. Because I told him that a gentleman like he really owed it to the world to make pure films so that he could be an example to all of the other film corporations and show the world what pure films were like. So Henry became very, very intreeged because he had never thought of the film profession before. So then I told him that we could get H. Gilbertson Montrose to write the senarios, and he to senshure them, and I could act in them and by the time we all got through, they would be a work of art. But they would even be purer than most works of art seem to be. So by the time we got to Philadelphia Henry said that he would do it, but he really did not think I had ought to act in them. But I told him from what I had seen of society women trying to break into the films, I did not believe that it would be so declasée if one of them really landed. So I even talked him into that.

So when we got to Henry's country estate, we told all of Henry's family and they were all delighted. Because it is the first time since the war that Henry's family have had anything definite to put their minds on. I mean Henry's sister really jumped at the idea because she said she would take charge of the studio trucks and keep them at a bed-rock figure. So I even promised Henry's mother that she could act in the films. I mean I even believe that we could put in a close-up of her from time to time, because after all, nearly every photoplay has to have some comedy relief. And I promised Henry's father that we would wheel him through the studio and let him look at all of the actresses and he nearly had another relapse. So then I called up Mr Montrose and made an appointment with him to meet Henry and talk it all over, and Mr Montrose, said, 'Bless you, little woman.'

So I am almost beginning to believe it, when everybody says I am nothing but sunshine because everybody I come into contract with always seems to become happy. I mean with the exception of Mr Eisman. Because when I got back to New York, I opened all of his cablegrams and I realized that he was due to arrive on the *Aquitania* the very next day. So I met him at the *Aquitania* and I took him to luncheon at the Ritz and I told him all about everything. So then he became very, very depressed because he said that just as soon as he had got me all educated, I had to go off and get married. But I told him that he really ought to be very proud of me, because in the future when he would see me at luncheon at the Ritz as the wife of the famous Henry H. Spoffard, I would always bow to him, if I saw him, and he could point me out to all of his friends and tell them that it was he, Gus Eisman himself, who educated me up to my station. So that cheered Mr Eisman up a lot and I really do not care what he says to his friends, because after all, his friends are not in my set, and whatever he says to them will not get around in my circle. So after our luncheon was all over, I really think that, even if Mr Eisman was not so happy, he could not help having a sort of a feeling of relief, especially when he thinks of all my shopping.

So after that came my wedding and all of the Society people in New York and Philadelphia came to my wedding and they were all so sweet to me, because practically every one of them has written a senario. And everybody says my wedding was very, very beautiful. I mean even Dorothy said it was very beautiful, only Dorothy said she had to concentrate her mind on the massacre of the Armenians to keep herself from laughing right out loud in everybody's face. But that only shows that not even Matrimony is sacred to a girl like Dorothy. And after the wedding was over, I overheard Dorothy talking to Mr Montrose and she was telling Mr Montrose that she thought that I would be great in the movies if he would write me a part that only had three expressions, Joy, Sorrow, and Indigestion. So I do not really believe that Dorothy is such a true friend after all.

So Henry and I did not go on any honeymoon because I told Henry that it really would be selfish for us to go off alone together, when all of our activities seemed to need us so much. Because, after all, I have to spend quite a lot of time with Mr Montrose going over the senario together because, Mr Montrose says I am full of nothing so much as ideas.

So, in order to give Henry something to do while Mr Montrose and I are working on the senario I got Henry to organize a Welfare League among all of the extra girls and get them to tell him all of their problems so he can give them all of his spiritual aid. And it has really been a very, very great success, because there is not much work going on at the other studios at present so all of the extra girls have nothing better to do and they all know that Henry will not give them a job at our studio unless they belong. So the worse they tell Henry they have been before they met him, the better he likes it and Dorothy says that she was at the studio yesterday and she says that if the senarios those extra girls have written around themselves to tell Henry could only be screened and gotten past the sensors, the movies would move right up out of their infancy.

So Henry says that I have opened up a whole new world for him and he has never been so happy in his life. And it really seems as if everyone I know has never been so happy in their lives. Because I make Henry let his father come to the studio every day because, after all, every studio has to have somebody who seems to be a pest, and in our case it might just as well be Henry's father. So I have given orders to all of the electricians not to drop any lights on him, but to let him have a good time because, after all, it is the first one he has had. And as far as Henry's mother is concerned, she is having her hair bobbed and her face lifted and getting ready to play Carmen because she saw a girl called Madam Calve play it when she was on her honeymoon and she has always really felt that she could do it better. So I do not discouradge her, but I let her go ahead and enjoy herself. But I am not going to bother to speak to the electricians about Henry's mother. And Henry's sister has never been so happy since the Battle of Verdun, because she has six trucks and 15 horses to look after and she says that the motion picture profession is the nearest thing to war that she has struck since the Armistice. And even Dorothy is very happy because Dorothy says that she has had more laughs this month than Eddie Cantor gets in a year. But when it comes to Mr Montrose, I really believe that he is happier than anybody else, because of all of the understanding and sympathy he seems to get out of me.

And so I am very happy myself because, after all, the greatest thing in life is to always be making everybody else happy. And so, while everybody is so happy, I really think it is a good time to finish my diary because after all, I am to busy going over my senarios with Mr Montrose, to keep up any other kind of literary work. And I am so busy bringing sunshine into the life of Henry that I really think, with everything else I seem to accomplish, it is all a girl had ought to try to do. And so I really think that I can say good-bye to my diary feeling that, after all, everything always turns out for the best.

...But Gentlemen Marry Brunettes

The Illuminating Diary of a Professional Lady

TO JOHN EMERSON

who discovered, developed, fostered and trained whatever I may have, if I have anything that is worth while.

Chapter One

I am going to begin a diary again, because I have quite a little time on my hands, with nothing to do for quite a time. I mean, in the first place I am full of ambitions and I think that practically every married girl ought to have a career if she is wealthy enough to have the home life carried on by the servants. Especially if a girl is married to a husband like Henry. Because Henry is quite a homebody and, if a girl was a homebody to, she would encounter him quite often. So that is why I try to do something in Life, and not let everything stop just because I have married the One of my choice. But I always believe in knowing several different kinds of people, and as long as my husband is of the wealthy classes, I prefer to meet brainy gentlemen who have got ideas on the outside. So I am practically always picking up something, and then when I go back and encounter Henry, I always have some new remark, or other, to make. For if Henry and I spent all of our time together neither of our ideas would be so bright. And it is bright ideas that keep the home fires burning, and prevent a divorce from taking all of the bloom off Romance.

So after Henry and I became married, the first career I started to have was the cinema. And we produced a superproduction based on sex life in the period of Dolly Madison. But when they wrote the scenario we had quite a little trouble, because the scenario writer wanted it to be full of nothing but "Psychology." And the director wanted it to be full of mob scenes and ornamental sets. And Henry wanted it to be full of a great moral lesson.

And I did not care what it was full of, so long as it was full of plenty of cute scenes where the leading man would chase me around the trunk of a tree and I would peek out at him, like Lillian Gish. So then Mr. Goldmark, the great film magnet, said, "Why not be on the safe side and have it full of everything?"

So the scenario turned out to be delightful, because it was not only a cute love story, but it was quite "Psychological," and it also taught a great moral lesson, and had very ornamental sets, in addition to a vialent mutiny in the Army. And it was really so full of everything that sometimes three or four things had to happen at once. For instants, the most psychological scene that Dolly Madison had, took place in the mother-of-pearl bathtub of an Executive Mansion, thinking of her Sweet-heart in double exposure, with the mutiny of the Army going on right outside the bathroom window.

Well, it seems that Dolly Madison was a Washington girl, so we had to go to Washington D. C. to take the scenes on account of historical acuracy. But it is quite difficult to take motion pictures in Washington, because, just when you select some delightful spot near the Capitol, and get everything all ready to take the scene, Senator Borrer or some other great man, would come up and plant himself in front of the camera. I mean, it is practically impossible to have a camera at Washington D. C. and keep great men away from the front of it. And, after all, those senators would have practically ruined the picture because, even if their costumes are quite quaint, they are not in the period of Dolly Madison. So I finally asked Dorothy to think up some good excuse to make them go away. And Dorothy told them that they would have to get out, because we were making a psychological picture, and their mental state had not yet reached the period of Dolly Madison. But I really think Dorothy could have used her brains and thought up a little more tack to use on Senators.

Well, when our cinema was finished the title turned out to be "Stronger than Sex," which was thought up by quite a bright girl in Mr. Goldmark's suite of offices. And the great moral lesson was, that girls could always help it, if they would only stop and think of Mother. And the close-up of me, where I stopped and thought of Mother, with a special lighting effect in blurred photography through a gauze screen, was really quite flattering. So we would have gone right on making more cinemas except for—"Something."

Because I am very fond of "kiddies" and when a girl has married a wealthy gentleman like Henry, Motherhood is even more beautiful, especially if it turns out to look like "Daddy." And even Dorothy says that "a kid that looks like any rich father is as good as money in the bank." I mean sometimes Dorothy becomes Philosophical, and says something that really makes a girl wonder how anyone who can make such a Philosophical remark can waste her time like Dorothy does.

And I always think that the sooner a girl becomes a Mother after the ceremony, the more likely it is to look like "Daddy." I mean, before a girl's mind gets concentrated on something else. But Dorothy said she would stop at one "kiddie" if she was I, because she thinks that one is enough of almost anything that looks like Henry. But Dorothy has no reverents for Motherhood.

So of course I had to give up the cinema, because I could not be as dishonest as one married cinema star I knew, who signed a contract to do quite a long serial, and did not tell the film corporation "her Secret." So before the serial was half finished, it began to become quite embarrassing to take scenes of her in the full length, because in the scenario she was only supposed to be a slip of an unmarried girl. So finally they had to start taking all of her scenes showing nothing but her head sticking up over the top of a bush or looking out of a window, and the result was that she got more close-ups than any film star ever got before.

But I do not think it is honorable to get close-ups by any such means as that.

Well after Henry heard about "my Secret," he had the idea to go and live at their old country estate where our "Little Mouse" could be born. Because "Little Mouse" was the nickname we thought up to call it by, until we found out what it was going to turn out to be. But I really preferred New York, so I told Henry that his whole family had been born in the suburbs of Philadelphia, so why not give our Little Mouse a chance? Because I read in a scientific medical book called "Waiting for the Little Stranger" that you should be where you can look at quite a lot of Art and have sweet thoughts and read nothing but beautiful poems and beautiful novels before it takes place. But Dorothy said I better slip in a page of Ring Lardner once in a while, or, if he was a boy, he might grow up to be a milliner. But anyway, I told Henry we ought to go to New York where all of the Art and Literature is.

But Henry said their own parlor in the suburbs of Philadelphia was practically full of Art, because his Father had spent years and years collecting nothing else. And there really *are* quite a lot of small size crockery statues of girls and their escorts getting ready to break into a minuette, with three glass show cases full of early period watches, to say nothing of the large marble statue of a full size baby having a bath with a real sponge in his hand, and seven piano lamps. So Henry said, why go to New York with all of that Art under my own roof? But I told Henry that the Art in our parlor was finished, but the Art of New York is still going on and you can meet great artists at their exhibitions and ask why they did it, and learn something.

But Henry thought he ought to stay where his Father was. Because Henry's Father is over 90, and Henry was trying to break him of quite a bad habit he had of making a new will every time a new nurse went on the case. And it does not seem to matter how unattractive a new nurse they are able to find, Henry's father can always weave a Romance around her. Until we sometimes wish that he would get well, or something.

And Henry's Mother is just as full of Romance as his Father. I mean when an elderly lady of 72 is always getting an idea that the butler is madly in love with her, it is quite difficult to keep in butlers. And Dorothy says that if we could only manage to get all the song writers to meet Henry's Mother, it would be the quickest way to free the world of Mother songs.

And as for Henry's sister, she and I have practically nothing that is common. I mean I do not mind boyish models on girls, if they copy some well groomed fashion plate, like "What the Young Man will Wear," for instants. But Ann Spoffard is the kind of a type that spends all of her time between a stable and a kennel, without having pressing done. I mean, I try to always think the best of everyone, and I really suppose it is quite unselfish for a girl to spend weeks and weeks washing a dog with mange cure, to cure *its* mange, and never give a thought to herself. But after all, she could be kind to *people* to, and make more use of O'de Calone before coming into the Salon.

So I finally had to put my brains to work to get Henry to move to New York. And when I put them to work I discovered that the *real* reason Henry wanted to stay in the suburbs of Philadelphia, was because he is quite promanent as long as he stays there, but by the time he arrives in New York he does not seem to be so unusual. Because, after all, to be promanent at New York, people have to be like Mr. Otto Kahn, for instants, who does quite a lot for Art, or else like the Reformers who do quite a lot against it. I mean Mr. Kahn can always make himself promanent by starting some artistic play, while any Reformer can make *himself* promanent by stopping one. But Henry never seems to have enough ideas to start anything, and even if it does not take any ideas to stop something, New York is full of such a lot of that kind of people that the competition is quite heavy.

And, the only thing that Henry can really do, is to talk against low morals. And he does not even seem to be able to make people repent, because the only ones who ever want to listen to that kind of conversation are people whose morals are pure and who only want to listen to it talked about. And the riskay things that Henry can think up may intreege the suberbs of Philadelphia, but they really would not be such a thrill in New York.

Well, of course when gentlemen from Kansas City or St. Louis come to New York and feel themselves becoming unpromanent, they can always make themselves very important by spending quite a lot of money on Head Waiters, and ticket speculaters, and the hostesses at night clubs. For practically anyone can call Texas Guynan by her first name for a few hundred dollars. But being promanent at Texas Guynan's would not really amuse Henry, unless he could go there and notice people enjoying themselves, and then be promanent in getting it closed up.

So I had to think quite hard to think up *some* way to make Henry feel promanent in New York and I decided that the quickest way was for him to jcin some associations.

So then I thought of a gentleman friend of mine in New York, who is very, very promanent, and belongs to practically everything, and I wrote him a letter and asked him if he could get some invitations for Henry to come to New York and belong to something, or other. So this gentleman belongs to the "Friends of Culture" and the "Nature Lovers Association" and "New York Distemper League," which is against dogs having distemper, and the "Ohio Society." And he got Henry an invitation to join everything, except the Ohio Society. Because it seems that the Ohio Society is very exclusive, because you have to be born in Ohio. But he got Henry an invitation to join the Pennsylvania Society, which is not so exclusive, because all you have to be born at is Pennsylvania.

Well, when Henry started in to receive all of those invitations, it made him feel very good to think that his promanents had reached New York. So he decided to go right up there and join everything that asked him. So of course he had to take me to. And when I got back into the Ritz again, after all of the home life I had been through, I almost believe I heaved a sigh.

Well the very first evening that Henry was in New York he went to a large banquet, and sat at the same table as Amy

Bottsfield Rand, who is very intelectual because she went to China once and can hardly bear anything since she came back, and Percy Gilchrist Saunders who is famous for thinking that spelling ought to sound like what it resembles, and Chester Wentworth Peabody who spends all of his time watching squirrels, and writes down every move they make. And meeting all of those famous people that New York is practically full of, gave Henry new thoughts, and opened up things. Because after Henry held a conversation with them, he was quite surprised to find out that he was just as full of brains as they were. But that is what always happens to people who have an inferior complex about coming to New York. Because no matter how inferior your complex is, you can always meet very promanent people in New York, who have not got any more brains than you have.

And when Henry came home from the banquet, I slipped into his bed room in my new pink negljay, and I finally got him to promise that we would live in New York, where our life could be more mental.

And so I gave Henry a supscription to the Book of the Month Club that tells you the book you have to read every month to make your individuality stand out. And it really is remarkable, because it makes over 50,000 people read the same book every month.

So then we took an apartment in the newest apartment house on Park Avenue, and I got nothing but the oldest antiques to go in it, with everything in antique Italian, and one of the oldest Rembrandts. I really almost have to smile, because I used to think that every interior ought to be decorated in pink satin with quite a lot of maribow. But after a girl has learned Art, she can hardly stand anything except old Italian. So instead of chiffon negljays with ostrich feather trimmings like I always used to wear, I wear nothing but antique Italian brocade, with a long train made out of some middle age embroidered Pope's robe with all of the faded colorings.

And when we did the nursery for the "Little Mouse," the interior decorator found a real genuine Italian cradle of one of the oldest centuries. But Dorothy said that the old Italian's idea when he made it, was that if the baby cashed in, the cradle was just the right shape for the funeral. And Dorothy was afraid that any baby that had to sleep in it, would grow up with a cute melancholy. I mean sometimes Dorothy does have quite a good idea, because it did turn out that an antique Italian apartment becomes quite depressing, especially on a rainy day. So I have Dorothy practically stay with us, to keep from becoming to depressed in such an antique Italian enviroment.

Well, the day finally came when the "Little Mouse" was due to arrive, and Dorothy and I were having luncheon at the Ritz. And after luncheon Dorothy was going shopping and then she was going to an informal tea. So she invited me to accompany her. Well, I am really fond of nothing as much as shopping, and even informal teas, but I finally decided I had better not go, so I went home instead. And when they put the "Little Mouse" in my arms that afternoon, I felt repayed for giving up everything.

But I called up Dorothy at the tea party to break her the news that it turned out to be a boy. Well, nothing touches people's hearts so much as a girl they are acquainted with, going through the "Valley of the Shadow," and coming out with a baby. So everybody at the tea wanted to come right over. And I sat up in bed, in my early Italian bed jacket, and we held quite a party to welcome the "Little Mouse." I mean people kept coming in, and coming in, and I had to keep telephoning Reubens to send over more sandwiches. But the nurse would only give us a small glimps of the "Little Mouse" because noise and cigarette smoke are not good for little babies the day of their arrival.

But, after all, I was repaid for going through all of those pangs, because Henry settled quite a large settlement on me. For nothing makes a husband become so sentimental in a financial way as the day he can call a girl "Little Mother."

Well after it was all over, of course Henry wanted me to stay at home and be nothing else but a Wife and Mother. And I really did not mind so long as I had to stay in bed anyway. But when I got out of bed, my brains started in to become active, and I began to think about a career. But I decided not to produce any more cinemas, because "Stronger Than Sex" went right over people's heads and became a financial failure. So I decided to become literary instead, and spend more time in some literary envirament, outside the home.

Chapter Two

Well, I soon found out that the most literary envirament in New York is the Algonquin Hotel, where all the literary geniuses eat their luncheon. Because every genius who eats his luncheon at the Algonquin Hotel is always writing that that is the place where all the great literary geniuses eat their luncheon. So I invited Dorothy to accompany me, and go there at luncheon time.

But Dorothy said that if I wanted to meet High Brows, she was going to a literary party that was being held by George Jean Nathan at a place in Jersey that is noted for serving the kind of beer that is made without ether. And Mr. H. L. Mencken, Theadore Dreiser, Sherwood Anderson, Sinclare Lewis, Joseph Hergesheimer and Ernest Boyd would be there. So I said to Dorothy "If they are so literary, why do they go to a place like New Jersey, which is chiefly noted for being inartistic?" And the only reason that Dorothy could think up, was on account of the *Beer*. But I finally decided to go, because some of them do write quite well-read novels.

But if anybody thinks that what they held in New Jersey was a literary salon, they would really be mistaken, because they did not even *mention* their literary work. And nobody ccculd have heard them if they had, because they kept putting nickels in an electric piano and breaking into riskay songs. And I think that when literary people wish to hold a musical evening, it is more artistic to buy tickets to some good opera. But I should have known enough to have my doubts about the literature of any literary gentlemen who have friendships with an unmental girl like Dorothy.

So the next day I made Dorothy go to luncheon at the Algonquin Hotel, and *that* made up for everything. For they are the *critics* who tell everybody else how to do it, and *they* know how to act. I mean, after all, they spend practically all their time showing everybody else how literary people ought to act.

Well we went to luncheon at the Algonquin hotel quite early, so that we could actually see them walk in. And I have learned that the best way to get a table near someone where you want to sit, is to become friendly with the head waiter. Well the famous head waiter at the Algonquin is called George, who holds a velvet rope across the doorway of a small exclusive dining room to keep people who do not apreciate genius from going where they do not belong. For they also have a more unexclusive dining room for the benefit of the masses. Well, I told George that we wished to sit near the famous literary Round-Table, where we could overhear them say something, or other. So George gave us the very nearest table of all, and the waiter who waited on us was the very one who waits on them, himself. So the waiter and I broke into a conversation, and it came out that his name was not only Tony, but he was full of ideals to. It really seems that the more I see of everybody, the more I realize that you never know who you are talking to. Because Tony told me that a man's body may only be a Greek waiter, but his soul may be full of all of the culture of the ancient Greeks themselves.

I mean it seems that Tony was raised to be a gentleman, because his father was quite a promanent Grecian who also had a son that was legitamate. So Tony's father put them both together and educated them by a tuter in all of the classics of the Grecian days. But Tony's father had become quite fed up with

Tony's mother, and so he got a Turkish chum of his to arrange for her to be present at an atrocity. It seems that the Turkish enjoy nothing so much as an atrocity, and Tony thinks it is the result of prohibition. Because the Turkish have always had prohibition, and Tony says that when things begin to get on a Turk's nerves, he cannot go out and have a drink and forget it, but he finally reaches the point where he has to do something vialent in a hurry. And Tony says that when he reads about the novel kind of murders we Americans can think up, and the enjoyable times we have at all of our murder trials, we Americans remind him quite a lot of the Turkish. So that is what made Tony think it is the result of prohibition.

So I paid Tony a compliment for his brains, in thinking things out. And Dorothy said she would pay him another one, for some chicken hash in a hurry. So he had to stop his conversation and go get it, because at luncheon time Dorothy's mind practically always runs on the subjeck of food, while I never seem to notice whether I am eating or not, so long as I am learning something.

Well when Tony came back I asked him to tell me all about the geniuses of the Round-Table. And it turned out that he knows them quite well, for they are all very fond of him. I mean, most waiters are more interested in tips, than they are in listening to geniuses converse, and the waiter that they had before Tony was quite a low Greek from Sardonopolis who had practically no interest in culture.

But Tony is different, and he listens with all his ears, and he hears even more than the geniuses do themselves, because they are so busy thinking up some cute remark to make next, that they never have time to do any listening.

Well the first genius who came in was Joel Crabtree, the great writer who writes a long collum every day on the subjeck of everything. I mean, providing it happened to some friend of his. Because it makes Mr. Crabtree feel very very good to have everybody think that *his* friends are greater geniuses than anybody elses friends. So the day never goes by, that every one of his friends are not mentioned in his literary collum, and all of the public that is interested in literature enough to read it, can find out what they have been doing every hour of the day or night. So naturally they are always trying to do something readable on purpose, like a match game of amuseing tideldywinks, or sharades at one anothers parties, or some laughable croquay championship in Central Park where you can draw quite a crowd with almost anything.

So then the famous critic of the drama came in, called Harry Appleby. And his job is to discover girls who remind him of Duse. And it is really quite difficult, because if you *discover* a girl, she naturally has to be quite young, and when a girl is so young she never seems to have as much techneek as Duse had. But Mr. Appleby always overlooks that point, if she is cute enough in other ways. Because there is nothing that this great critic of the drama loves so much as an actress, or even an actor, being cute. And if a play is cute in addition, he feels that the heighth of drama has occurred at last. So Tony loves to listen to Mr. Appleby, and then he writes to his cousin at Athens, that he has practically been listening to Sofacles. I mean he has to mention names that his cousin can understand, because Tony says his cousin is an ignorant fellow, and he would no more know that Mr. Appleby was a famous genius at the Algonquin, than Mr. Appleby would know that Sofacles was a famous genius at Greece.

And the next literary genius who came in, was Peter Hood, the writer, who is always falling in love with some new girl. And when a genius falls in love with a lady genius, Tony says, "there is h—— to pay," because he cannot go off and have an affair and keep his mouth shut like a waiter, but he has to talk it over with his wife, and then they have to look it up in Psychoanalisis, and then they have to talk it all over with all of the other geniuses, and they really never get to any conclusion on the subjeck.

Well finally all of the geniuses were present at last, and the way the conversation worked out was really remarkable. Because, first one genius said to another, "What was that screamingly funny remark you made last Tuesday?" So then *he* told it and they all laughed. And then it was *his* turn to ask, "And what was that terribly clever thing *you* said on Friday?" So then the other genius got *his* chance, and it was all give-and-take, so that everybody had an opportunity to talk about himself.

But then Mr. Ernest Boyd came in and sat right down at their table. And I am sure that he was not welcome, because he was the one at Mr. Nathan's party in New Jersey who rendered the most unrefined song of the whole evening. So how could *he* appreciate the kind of conversation they hold at the Algonquin? But he really seemed to laugh louder than anyone. I mean he even laughed when nobody else did, and they finally had to cast dark looks in his direction.

So then they all started to tell about a famous trip they took to Europe. And they had a marvellous time, because everywhere they went, they would sit in the hotel, and play cute games and tell reminiscences about the Algonquin. And I think it is wonderful to have so many internal resources that you never have to bother to go outside of yourself to see anything.

So then Mr. Boyd spoke up and asked "What fellow-literatours did you meet on your trip abroad?" I mean Mr. Boyd does not know the etiquet of holding a conversation, and he kept asking questions that had very little reply.

But it turned out that one of them did have a letter to a literatour called James Joyce, but he did not bother to present it, because he said, after all, James Joyce did not know who *he* was, and why bother to meet somebody who knew so little about the "Algonquin" that he probably would think it meant a tribe of uncivilized Indians. But Mr. Boyd went right on and said, "Why didn't you take a sporting chance and meet him? He might have had something to say."

So then they told Mr. Boyd, that every time they met somebody new, they had to stop and explain all of their personal illusions before their jokes could be laughed at, and it only wasted everybody's time. And I really do not know why the geniuses at the Algonquin should bother to learn about Europe any more than Europe bothers to learn about them. So they came back, because they like the Algonquin best after all. And I think it is remarkable, because the old Proberb tells about the Profit who was without honor in his own home. But with them it is just the reverse.

Well, Dorothy finally finished her chicken hash and spoke up and said that she had overheard enough intellectual conversation for one day, so she was going out to hunt up a friend of hers who only talks about himself when he has a toothache.

And I was really glad she went. Because then something happened that was really embarrassing, but it ended by becoming one of the greatest thrills of my Life. I mean Mr. Boyd looked over and noticed me, so of course I had to throw him a smile. And then he turned and addressed the whole Round-Table, and said "Gentlemen you are always discovering a Duse, or a Sapho or a Cleopatra every week, and I think it is my turn. Because I have discovered a young lady who is all three rolled into one. May I have the permission to bring Mrs. Henry Spoffard over to the table?" Well, they really pay very little attention to anything Mr. Boyd says, but they said they did not mind. So he escorted me over to their table and introduced me, and almost all of them nodded to me, and some of them even spoke. And they let me sit there until luncheon was all over.

Well, Mr. Hood noted my reverants for everything they said and he finally told me that he realized I had more in me than I looked, so he issued me an invitation to come to luncheon every day. And I really would not be surprised, from the way he acted, if *I* turned out to be the next one to end up in a Psychoanalisis with Mr. Hood. And when I told Dorothy, she said it would do him a world of good, because I would know what to do in such a case, and he would get somewheres at LAST. So I may even turn out to be similar to the great Inspirations of history.

Well, the next thing I had to do was to join the Lucy Stone League, so that I could keep my own maiden name after matrimony. Because a girl's name should be Sacred, and when she uses her husband's it only sinks her identity. And when a girl always insists on her own maiden name, with vialents, it lets people know that she must be important some place or other.

And quite a good place to insist on an unmarried name, is when you go to some strange hotel accompanied by a husband. Because when the room clerck notes that a girl with a maiden name is in the same room with a gentleman, it starts quite a little explanation, and makes a girl feel quite promanent before everybody in the lobby.

But Dorothy said I had better be careful. I mean she says that most Lucy Stoners do not *really* worry the room clerck, because they are generally the type that are only brought to hotels on account of matrimony. But Dorothy said that when Henry and I waltz in and ask for a room with my maiden name the clerck would probably take one good look at me, and hand Henry a room in the local jail for the Man act.

But I do not listen to any advice about literature from a girl like Dorothy. And so I joined it. And now I can write my book without my identity being sunk by having the name of a husband to crush me.

Chapter Three

Well, when I finally became literary, I decided that I would not be the kind of an authoress who leaves the world no better off than it was in the first place, by being destructive, but I would always try to teach some lesson, that would make it even better. And the best lesson I have ever come in contract with, is the life of my girl friend Dorothy. So I decided to write about that. Only the life of Dorothy is not going to be so much for girls to resemble, as it is to give them a warning what they should stop doing.

I mean, in the first place, Dorothy was born in quite a low envirament. And a low envirament is all very cute in the cinema, for Mary Pickford can be rescued out of even an ash can, and still turn out refreshing at the finish by marrying some wealthy millionaire. But although Dorothy has improved her envirament from quite a low one to the Ritz hotel, even living at the Ritz has not improved Dorothy's ideals, for she does nothing but fall madly in love with the kind of gentlemen who were born without money and have not made any since.

Well, when I told Henry that I was going to write the life of Dorothy, we had quite a little quarrel. Because Henry seemed to think that the world would only be the better off for *not* knowing the life of a girl like Dorothy. I mean, Henry is quite broad minded like all great Reformers have to be in order to look at both sides of the same thing at once. And he really does not mind what a girl has been through, as long as she does not enjoy herself at the finish. But Henry said that when girls like Dorothy do not pay, and pay, how are all the moral people going to get their satisfaction out of watching them suffer. And what would happen to Christianity?

But I finally persuaded Henry to let me write it, for I said that he could read it all over, and give it a sanction before it ever reached the public. So if it *does* reach the public it means that girls can know with safety before they begin to read that they are going to learn something to their advantage.

Well, the first thing that Dorothy remembers about her Life was when she was a small child, she and her Father belonged to what was known as the "Greater Pacific Street Fair and Carnaval Company" on the Pacific Coast. Because it seems that whenever the Knites of Pithias or the Lithuanian Church in some small size town, wish to hold a carnaval for the benefit of something, they communicate with companies that make a profession of doing nothing but travel around and hold carnavals. And these companies are only supposed to supply the merry go rounds and freaks and kewpie dolls, but I *think* their real profession lies in deceeving the public. Because Dorothy says that after the benefit was over, the Knites of Pithias or the Lithuanian church would be in such a crippled financial condition that they could not afford another benefit for years and years.

Well it seems that in every Carnaval Company there is some gentleman who does something free, to amuse or instruct the public, like wearing pink spangel tights for instants, and jumping off the Post Office roof into a tank full of water. And the one who did that in their Carnaval Company, was nobody less than Dorothy's Father, Mr. Shaw. So I had to ask Dorothy, if her Father never came to grief doing such an occupation? And it seems that one time he *did* have quite a little accident, because he was always in a cronik state of being intoxicated, and he made a mistake in the hour, and jumped off the Post Office roof before they had filled the tank yet. But Dorothy says it didn't hurt him much, because it was just a case of 'tank meet tank," and her Father had enough in *him* to make up for the other one being empty.

Well it seems that while Dorothy's Father was jumping off roofs, Dorothy's Mother spent her time in quite an expensive flat at San Francisco. But she was so undomestic that she could hardly stand anything in the way of a husband, although every once in a while she would suddenly get quite Maternal, and send for Dorothy. So then Dorothy's Father would put her on the train to San Francisco, in the charge of some railroad conductor.

And Dorothy's Mother would meet her at the Station, with a wealthy gentleman acquaintance of hers who seemed to be inseparable. And they would be all enthusiasm over Dorothy and buy her delightful clothes and take her out to the races, and road houses and show her off to everybody, and drink her "health" in champagne. But in the midst of some party, Dorothy's Mother and her gentleman friend would gradually begin to lose all of their Maternal instincks, and they would finally end up by sending Dorothy back to the flat in charge of a messenger boy. And then Dorothy's Mother would neglect coming home herself, and Dorothy would be left alone for days in the flat with a Chinaman cook who did nothing but mark Chinese lottery tickets, that might just as well have been Greek to a small child of Dorothy's age. So Dorothy would be more than delighted when her Mother finally remembered to come home and send her back to the Carnaval Company.

Well when Dorothy was about 12 years of age, her Father received a telegram that his wife had suddenly passed away when the grand stand collapsed at the Tia Wanna race track. And Dorothy says the only bet her Father ever won on the races, was when he bet that a promanent San Francisco millionaire was also among the casualty. Because it turned out that he was, and that was the end of Dorothy's Mother. But I do not think that Dorothy's Mother was all that she should be, or she would not have allowed the kitchen help to indulge in lotteries.

Well, by the time Dorothy was 14 she could always go round here and there in the fair grounds and lead a helping hand. Because they had what is called "concessions" which means people would throw rings at a lot of knives, for instants, and the one who really did it, won the knife. So Dorothy would mix up with the crowd and be the One that won the knife. And then she would go around to the rear, and give the knife back to the gentleman who ran the concession. Because Dorothy says, after all, the knifes cost nearly two dollars a gross, so what was the use of wasting them? But I told Dorothy that that is what I would call cheating the Public, but Dorothy says it wasn't cheating them so much, because the blades of the knifes were only made out of tin foil anyway, and would do nobody any good who was interested in cutting.

Well finally when Dorothy became about the age of 15, her Father came to grief. I mean Mr. Shaw had to get married again. And it is quite an interesting story that seemed to occur because of the main attraction of the Carnaval Company, that was called "The Lover's Leap."

Well, this Lover's Leap consisted of a track which was in the shape of a large "Loop-the-Loop," with a small automobile that ran on it. So after the automobile had "looped-the-loop," it took quite a long jump in the air and landed on quite a high landing at quite a long distants. But what really intreeged the Public was the Blonde Girl in a linen duster that sat in it. For this girl was supposed to be looping-the-loop in order to meet her "Lover." And her "Lover" was nobody else but Mr. Shaw in his pink spangel tights, who stood waiting in a pose on the landing and showed her down the steps with galantry, while the applause would be deffening. But Dorothy says she never did find out whether they were applauding the Lover's Leap of the girl, or the fact that her Father managed to reach the bottom of the steps in his condition.

Well, in order to get blonde girls to ride in the Lover's Leap, the Carnaval Company would generaly make use of a stage struck waitress with a blonde wig on. But they had quite a lot of difficulty keeping in waitresses, because after a waitress had made a few Lover's Leaps, her back bone would start in to colapse. So then it would become necessary for the Manager of the Carnaval Company to start associating with fresh waitresses, in order to pick up another.

Well finally in the hotel at a town called Modesto, the Manager picked up a waitress who did not tell him that her Mother was the landlady of the hotel. Because it seems that this waitress was afraid that he would not give her the engagement, if he knew that she had quite a vialent Mother who was opposed to a career. So this waitress, who was called Hazel, ran away with the Carnaval Company without notifying her Mother. And to make things even worse, it seems that some of the Carnaval Company left the hotel without notifying the clerck to make out their bill.

Well, the Landlady arrived on the scene at the next town and Dorothy says that when she showed up she had blood in her eye. But as Fate would have it, she reached Main Street just as Dorothy's Father was jumping off the Masonic Temple in his pink spangel tights. And although that Landlady had never paid Mr. Shaw any attention when he was stopping at her own hotel in sivilian clothes, it seems that the moment she saw him dashing off a roof in tights, she fell madly in love.

Well, it finally became necessary for the Management to hold conferences with Hazel's Mother. But from the very first, it soon became aparent that nothing would apease her, but to marry Mr. Shaw. Well Dorothy's Father had to do it, to save the Carnaval Company from the charge of abducking a waitress, and non-paying of hotel bills. So they were married by the Lutheran minister, and had quite a novel wedding in a lion's cage, and that was the way Dorothy came to have a Step-Mother.

Well, the first thing that Dorothy's Step-Mother did, was to make Hazel go back home to look out for the hotel in Modesto, because she considered that life in a Carnaval Company would be hard on Hazel's morals. But Dorothy says that Hazel's morals had had wear and tear enough right in Modesto to take the novelty out of anything she could learn in a Carnaval Company.

But Dorothy's Step-Mother staid with the Carnaval Company and turned out to be nothing but a termagint. I mean she never allowed Mr. Shaw to jump off any more roofs, and he began to lose all of his personality. And it finally reached the point where all Mr. Shaw could do to amuse or instruct the public was to take out a marriage license in every town they went to, and be married in public, in a baloon, or a cage full of tigers, to Mrs. Shaw by the local minister. So Dorothy says, if I ever hear anybody make any cracks about her having a Father who was not a marrying man, to just tell them that *her Father* held the record of the entire Pacific Coast for the number of times he was legally married.

But things finally went from bad to worse. Because, even though Mrs. Shaw was constantly a bride, her actions failed to show it. And she did nothing but disaprove of the bridegroom, even at the alter, so that sometimes the crowd at the wedding would really wonder what Mr. Shaw saw in her. For Dorothy says that hardly anybody wants to pay a quarter to see somebody get married to a pesamistic bride who is nearing the age of 50.

But I do not really blame Mrs. Shaw for becoming discouraged because, after all, Dorothy's Father was never an ideal husband. I mean he seemed to think it was an accomplishment to become intoxicated even before prohibition was dreamed of. So Mrs. Shaw began to get very "fed up" with the life of a Carnaval Company and began to yearn for her own hotel, especially when she got news that it was beginning to have a bad name. Because it seems that hardly any comercial traveler who had pretentions to any good looks, ever paid Hazel his bill. And when Dorothy's Step-Mother heard that Hazel had changed the breakfast hour from 6.30 to 8, she decided that things had gone far enough. So she made Mr. Shaw renounce his whole career, in order to be taken back and kept at the Mansion House in Modesto.

Well, Dorothy's Step-Mother offered to take Dorothy with them, but Dorothy thought it over, and decided not to go. Because Dorothy says that she might have been able to stand either Hazel, or her Step-Mother, or Modesto separately, but a combination of all three was beyond human endurance.

Well, of course, *now* Dorothy had to begin to earn her own living. So the Carnaval Company took up a collection and bought her a nickel plated waffle machine, and the Manager told Dorothy that she need not pay for the concession of running it, until it was on a paying basis.

So then it was arranged that Dorothy would live under the chaperonage of Mr. and Mrs. Al Le Vino who owned a concession called "The Temple of Art" which was a tent where Mr. Le Vino sang illustrated songs and threw illustrated song slides on his wife in white tights with long sleeves like a butterfly. And the home life of Mr. and Mrs. Le Vino was ideal, because they did not go to a hotel like the rest of the Carnaval Company, but they kept house right in their own tent on account of being domestically inclined. And Dorothy says that she wishes sometimes that some banquet at the Colony restaurant would be delicious enough to make her forget the memory of Mrs. Le Vino's stew. And the only trouble with the Le Vino's was, that after seventeen years of married life they still talked baby talk to each other and sooner or later, it was bound to get on Dorothy's nerves.

Well, after Dorothy was settled, she and her Father said good-bye, and he was taken off to be nagged at in Modesto. And he is out there yet, living with Mrs. Shaw at the Mansion House and drownding his feelings as best as he can in the days of Prohibition. And the greatest comfort he has is Hazel's husband. Because Hazel turned out quite well and got married, and Dorothy says the only trouble with Hazel was, that she was ahead of her time. I mean, nowadays all the other flappers have caught up with Hazel, and it only goes to show that she was nothing but a premature debutant after all. And she married the "catch" of Modesto, who runs a newspaper office. And all of the farmers pay Hazel's husband their bills in either grapes or Bohemian hops. So Mr. Shaw and Hazel's husband love to mess about with them in the back room of the printing office, and see what they can get. And only last month, on his birthday,

Dorothy sent her Father the finest copper still that money could buy.

Well, when the waffle machine arrived at the Carnaval Company it had a little pamflet inside saying that "even a child could operate it." And that gave Dorothy an idea, so she used to turn the waffle machine over to some small size local boy of the town, who was always more than delighted. But the result was, that the waffle machine was generally laid away for repares, or the small boy ate up all the profits.

Well, finally at a town called San Diego, trouble overtook the Carnaval Company. And it was all on account of a member who was called Doc. And Doc sold a thing that was called "Miracle Spot Eradicator" which was made by buying a cake of laundry soap for five cents at the corner grocery store, and cutting it up in small size pieces, and selling it to the Public for 25 cents each wrapped up in tin foil.

But it seems that Doc was practically always doing wrong, and he had left a trail of disturbed husbands clear across the State of California. And what finally got him into trouble at last, was that he not only sold a grocer's wife in San Diego $4 worth of Miracle Spot Eradicator that he had just bought from her own husband for a nickel, but he took advantage of her in addition, and stole the grocer's watch off the bedroom cheffoneer. And the watch was worth $75, so it made the grocer angry, and he reported Doc to the authorities.

Well, a Deputy Sherif of San Diego started on the trail, and caught up with the Carnival Company at a town called Santa Barbera. And it seems that this Deputy Sherif was quite a famous character, because he not only came from quite a wealthy old family, but he also took a very great Public interest in the morals of young girls who were on the verge of womanhood. And he was very promanent on the board of directors of the Detention Home, and the main reason that he was interested in the case of the grocer's wife, was because she was a graduate from there, and the low state of her morals always seemed to intreeg him.

Well the Deputy Sherif arrived at the Fair Grounds in Santa

Barbara quite early in the morning, before any of the crowd was there, and noted Dorothy sitting under the front flap of the Le Vino's tent, watching Mrs. Le Vino crochay a boudoire cap. Well, he came up to Mrs. Le Vino to inquire about Doc, but his gaze seemed to wander more toward Dorothy. And practically from that moment, it soon became aparent that while his official position might be hounding Doc to Justice, in a personal way his mind was running more on Dorothy. And as time went on, he practically blinked his eyes at Doc, and Doc really got so bold that he became more and more of a lady's man, and flaunted his Eradicator right and left. While the Deputy Sherif's principal idea seemed to be to get Dorothy off in some corner, and tell her that she had reached the point where it was time for somebody moral, like him, to help her get from Girlhood into Womanhood.

And it really does seem remarkable that Dorothy had reached the age of 16 in a Carnaval Company, without the subjeck of "Life" being brought to her notice. Because when I was only 13, I sang in our church quire, and practically every boy in our quire had at least mentioned the subjeck, and some of them had even done more. But it seems that the enviroment of a Carnaval Company is not so much like a church quire. Because in a Carnaval Company, nothing is Sacred, and they all went out of their way to make jokes about "Love" in front of Dorothy, so that Dorothy would laugh it off. But Love is so Sacred in a church quire, that they never even mention it above a whisper, and it becomes more of a mistery. And when a thing is a mistery, it is always more intreeging. So there was quite a lot more Love going on in our church quire, than there was in Dorothy's Carnaval Company, where nothing was Sacred. So Dorothy's whole attitude about the subjeck was quite irreverant, at a time when she should have been worrying about the problems of a young girl, and thinking about Life and *wondering*.

Chapter Four

Well, I always think that when a young girl of 16 is thoughtless about what is going to happen to her in a Carnaval Company, she is beginning to start toward the edge of a brink.

And it seems that Dorothy had already made a chum out of the company's snake eater who went by the knick name of Curley. So when she had to choose between the attentions of a wealthy Deputy Sherif and the company of someone whose financial condition consisted of a box full of eating snakes, Dorothy never hesitated to do the wrong thing. And finally the Deputy Sherif became worried about Dorothy, and went to Curley himself, and told him that he ought to be ashamed to be constantly seen with a young girl who was just beginning to blossom, because it was putting Evil thoughts into everybody's mind.

Well, Curley blushed very much, for a snake eater. But he told the Deputy Sherif that he and Dorothy put in all of their time "having laughs" together, so he had never thought about Evil. But Curley thanked the Deputy Sherif for putting it into his mind and promised that he would try to do better in the future. And the result was that the next time Curley incountered Dorothy, he looked at her and looked at her with quite a new look, and he finally remarked, "Well, Mug, I guess you're grown up!"

Well, it seems that part of Curley's occupation in the Carnaval Company was to take a lot of hand-bills advertising the Street Fair to the fartherest corner of every town and litter up the sidewalks with them. So this day it happened to be spring time, and the weather was delightful. So Curley invited Dorothy to go along to. But when they reached the residential quarter, he threw all of the hand-bills in an ash can, and invited Dorothy to take a walk in the country instead.

Well, they took a street car and got off at the end of the line, in the country. And the sun was shining and the sky was full of beautiful birds, and the grass was full of beautiful vialets, and the envirament would have made almost anybody think about Love, except a girl like Dorothy. I mean, she is just the opasite to a girl like I, because when I am alone with a gentleman, in almost any envirament, I always keep in mind that something might happen.

Well, finally Curley began to ask Dorothy, in quite an off-hand manner, what she thought of the home life of Mr. and Mrs. Al Le Vino? Because it seems that Curley thought it was ideal, even if it did take place in a tent. But Dorothy told Curley that was because he did not have to live in the tent with them. Because, as far as she was concerned, she had just about reached the end of her endurants, and some day when Al Le Vino called Pearl Le Vino "lambie pie" for the 29th time in one day, she was going to make vialent use of a rock.

Well, then Curley tried to explane to Dorothy that practically everybody feels like the Le Vinos some time in their life, and the only difference between the Le Vinos and everybody else was, that Le Vinos went right on feeling that way. But Dorothy told Curley that if he ever noticed *her* getting into any such a condition, she hoped he would train one of his snakes to bite her.

Well, then Curley held his tongue for quite a while. But after a while, he told Dorothy he supposed, after all, that she was to young to be talking about any such a matter yet, so they might just as well go back to the Fair Grounds.

But all the way back to the Fair Grounds, Curley seemed to be quite depressed, because he never spoke a word. And then Dorothy started in to think. And then Dorothy says she started in to wonder if she would ever reach the point of falling in love with somebody, and be just as disgusting as Pearl Le Vino.

Well, after all, it was Spring time, and the wild vialets smelled quite a lot, and Dorothy says that finally she began to wonder what it would be like to have some big bozo grap you and give you a good smack. And such a way of putting it only shows how Dorothy's thoughts can be unrefined, even on the subjeck of Love.

Well, Dorothy kept on thinking until she says she finally came to a conclusion that she had heard so much about that "Love" racket that it was about time she gave it a whirl, and found out for herself if it had been over-advertised. And I really suppose you could not blame Dorothy for being skeptical, because she had spent her whole life among people who advertised to eat snakes or give away jack knives, and never lived up to their advertisement.

Well, when Dorothy decided to do it, she says that the only one she could think of who would be interested, was the Deputy Sherif, for Curley never entered her mind as "Romance." And by the time they got back to the Fair Grounds, the Deputy Sherif was there, as usual, sitting under the back flap of the Le Vino's tent, making a pretents of helping Mrs. Le Vino shell peas, but in reality he was looking in all directions for Dorothy. So, as long as Dorothy had made up her mind to find out about "Things," she got rid of Curley and gave the Deputy Sherif a kind word, for the first time since he had started to follow the Carnaval Company. And she ended up by making an engagement to go to the cinema in town with him that night.

So when night time came, Dorothy deserted the waffle machine, as usual, and went to town with the Deputy Sherif. And it was really quite a co-instance, for the cinema was all about Love, and the electrik piano played "Kiss Me Again," and Dorothy finally reached the point where she decided to let the Deputy Sherif hold her hand. And Dorothy says that she would give a dollar to know what *he* got out of it, because as far as she was concerned, she had just as soon hold one of her own waffles that got left out in the rain. So Dorothy kept saying to herself, "It has got to be a h—— of a lot better than this, or the Le Vinos haven't got a leg to stand on!"

But Dorothy decided not to be hasty until she had given the experiment a good trial, and she made up her mind that before she got through that night, she would let the Deputy Sherif kiss her.

Well, by the time they walked back to the Fair Grounds, everything was deserted, and it was quite dark except for the moonlight. So they stopped in front of the Le Vino's tent, and Dorothy says she let the Deputy Sherif rant on about how beautiful Girlhood was, especially when a girl started in to get toward Womanhood. So when he finished talking himself out, she gritted her teeth and let the Deputy Sherif kiss her. And after it was all over, Dorothy says she felt like a little boy who had just found out that Santy Clause was the Sunday School Superintendent.

Well, it seems that all of the time Curley was hiding behind the tent, waiting to see if Dorothy got home safe, and when she let the Deputy Sherif kiss her, he stepped out and told Dorothy to get to bed, quite harshly! And then Curley held a long conversation, walking around the Fair Grounds in the dark, with the Deputy Sherif.

Well, the next morning the Deputy Sherif apeared and told Mrs. Le Vino that he had telegraphed for his Mother to come and get Dorothy and that he and his Mother would take her to their home in San Diego, and send her to school, and when she was educated up to it, they would see what they would see, because his object was Matrimony.

Well, when Dorothy heard the news she realized that it was nothing but the work of Curley. So she went to hunt him up and found him sitting alone in his canvas snake pit. So Dorothy says she started to give him h—— for making an old lady like the Deputy Sherif's Mother take a long ride on a railroad train for a joke that was not even funny, because Dorothy could not even imagine going away with that Deputy Sherif.

Well, then it became Curley's turn to give Dorothy an arguement. And he told her that, even if she had not noticed it, all of her friends in the Carnaval Company worried about her a lot. Because it seems that she had turned out to be nothing but a Problem. And, as far as Curley himself was concerned, he had just about given up the answer. Because how any girl could hold such an innacent conversation with him about "Life" in the morning, and then go for that Deputy Sherif the way Dorothy went for him the very same night in the dark, almost made Curley believe that he did not understand women. And Dorothy tried her best to think up an explanation, but there did not seem to be any.

So then Curley said that, anyway, Dorothy ought to be learning about Morals, and he had begun to realize that a Carnaval Company was no place to do it in. Because hardly anything they did in a Carnaval Company was honest. And even Dorothy herself, had gotten in the habit of stealing the bill posters paste, to make waffles out of, which was no foundation for any young girl's character.

So then Curley went on to say that he did not think a great deal of the Deputy Sherif's brain power, but anyway he was promanent and wealthy, and a young girl would be safe with his Mother, or Al Le Vino's illustrated songs had given him a bum steer. So Curley told Dorothy she must show apreciation, and go with them for a couple of years and learn Truth and Honesty and then, if she could not stand them any longer, she could always run away and give them the slip.

Well, Dorothy begged Curley and begged him, to let her stay with the Carnaval Company, and she promised that she would reform, and even put an egg in the waffle dough.

But then it came out that Curley himself was leaving the Carnaval Company. Because it seems that Curley had begun to realize that Snake Eating hardly ever got anyone anywhere, and he said that if he had only thought of it before, he might have done differently, and he might have had something to offer a girl himself. But he said that he had sent $3 to Kansas

City, for a thousand German whetstones, and as soon as they arrived, he was going to strike out alone in the world and make a Man of himself.

Well, when Dorothy heard that Curley was going to leave, she realized that her Street Fair days were over, because she could not stand living with the Le Vinos without any comic relief. So everything seemed to work out toward one end and Dorothy finally had to promise Curley that she would wait for the Deputy Sherif's Mother, and look her over and, if they seemed to be able to stand each other, she would give it a trial.

But it seemed quite peculiar that all of the time the Deputy Sherif kept trying to get Dorothy back of some tent or other, and give her talks. And Dorothy says she never listened to such a conglomeration of Religion and poetry spoken by a man who couldn't keep his hands off a girl. And Dorothy did not know whether to mention it to Curley or not, but she was so ashamed of being such a Problem that she decided she ought not to make people any more trouble.

Well, the morning the Deputy Sherif's Mother arrived, Dorothy, Curley, the Le Vinos, and the Deputy Sherif went down to the station to meet her. And when she got off of the train, she turned out to be a small size lady, who looked quite harmless. And the Deputy Sheriff rushed up, and grabbed her and kissed and kissed her. And Dorothy said that the way he went on about a "Mother" would have made an Irish tenor sound like an ungrateful son.

And it turned out that the whole Carnaval Company were more than delighted with her, because nothing touches the heart of a Carnaval Company like somebody's Mother. And Al Le Vino went from one concession to another, telling everybody, in quite a hearty voice, that "the Deputy Sherif's Mother was a *Sweetheart*!" So that very afternoon the Deputy Sherif went out and arrested Doc at last and everything was ready to start for San Diego the next day.

Well, the Carnaval Company felt quite depressed because Dorothy had been with them for years. And they gave her a going away party, in the Main Tent, with Pearl Le Vino's home made cake and lemonade and a going-away present of a large size Bible to show a Deputy Sherif's Mother what kind of people they have in a Carnaval Company.

And they all cried, and kissed Dorothy and became quite sentamental on the subjeck of "a Mother." And they gave Dorothy good advice, to always do what "Mother" said. But Dorothy seemed to note that the Deputy Sherif talked so much that his Mother never got a chance to say *anything*. But so long as everybody was so full of satisfaction, Dorothy did not like to spoil their fun by making remarks. So she held her tongue, and before she hardly knew it, it was almost train time to be taken away to San Diego. And then Dorothy realized at last, that she had to say goodbye to Curley. So Curley asked Dorothy to sneak out of the back flap with him and they held their last conversation together.

Well, Curley made Dorothy walk towards the snake pit, in quite an off hand manner, and when he got Dorothy alone in there, he presented her with a going-away present of an Armadillo basket. And an Armadillo basket is the shell of a small size animal that is born at Texas, in sections like the elbow of a stove pipe, and is lined in serise china silk with a ribbon running from his nose to his tail to make the handel, and Dorothy had wanted one for years. But I think it is very very cruel to kill all the little Armadillos to make Armadillo baskets, because I always think that people ought not to kill little animals unless they get something useful, like at least an ermin coat.

Well, Dorothy thanked Curley for the Armadillo basket and then she told him that she wanted him to except her nickel plated waffle machine, so that he could sell it, and buy himself a going-away present of a folding stand to sell German whetstones off of, to remember her by.

But Curley asked Dorothy what kind of a MAN he would make out of himself if he started in by excepting a present from a girl? And he told her that he had made up his mind to begin selling them off of the sidewalk and work his way up.

Well, suddenly they heard everybody calling "Dorothy" in a loud tone of voice, because it was getting late for train time. So they had to run out and be hurried to the station and everything was such confusion of getting on board and saying goodbye, with all of Dorothy's bundles and the Armadillo basket, that Dorothy can only remember Curley when he stood on the steps of the railroad train saying "So long Pal! If I never see you again, always remember that I think you're *Hell*!" And then he had to jump off, because the train was going away.

But there was quite a peculiar look on Curley's face, so when Dorothy went into the car, she sat down in a seat by the Deputy Sherif's Mother, and began to have her own thoughts. And it suddenly came over Dorothy like a flash that Curley was in Love with her. And to think that somebody she had always admired in such a viril way, had gone and become soft like Al Le Vino, almost made Dorothy sick to her stomach.

Chapter Five

Well, Dorothy had the opertunity to settle down and forget the past in a small size city, where life is pure and people's thoughts are wholesome without contamination. And, when they arrived there at San Diego, the Deputy Sherif escorted Doc to Jail, while his Mother escorted Dorothy to their old family residents. And when they reached it, it turned out to be a very beautiful large wooden house of the impressive type, with six pointed cupalows on the roof, built out of fancy scalloped shingles by their ancestors. And when Dorothy was shown to her room, it had one of the cupalows in the corner for a large bay window, with dotted swiss ruffle curtains and there were roses all over the wall paper and an anteek what-not, with a picture of George Washington saying his prayers in a snow drift over an old original walnut bedstead. But when the Deputy Sherif's Mother left her alone in it, Dorothy says the atmosphere of that room made a girl wish that somebody would mail her a pie, with a file and a rope ladder in it.

Well, finally a servant girl, called Emma, knocked on the door, and asked Dorothy if she could help her unpack. So Dorothy invited her in, and while they were unpacking, Dorothy started to ask her quite a few questions.

Well, it turned out that Emma was a graduate of the Detention Home. Because the Deputy Sherif loved nothing so much as giving imoral girls a new start, and keeping in touch with their cases. But Emma said that some day he was going to keep in touch with her case just once to often! And when she said it, quite a dark expression came over her countenance. So Emma did not cheer Dorothy up so much, and Dorothy would have given anything if she had not promised Curley her word of honor that she would stick it out for a year.

Well, when Dorothy went down stairs she found out that the Deputy Sherif's Mother had just as little to say when she had an opertunity to say it, as when the Deputy Sherif would not let her get a word in edgewise. Because living with such a promanent son had sapped her vitality.

But finally it came dinner time, and the Deputy Sherif arrived home with a Guest he had invited. And this Guest was a bleach blonde Secretary of quite a middle age, who had started out in his office years ago, when she was only a typewriter. And it seems that in the beginning there had been a "Romance." And even after the Romance was over, they kept on going through quite a few things together. Like one time, when he constructed some city construction and put decomposed granite where he should have put marble, this Secretary had kept all of his books on the subjeck, and she was so full of information that he really felt as if he could hardly get along without her. And he never dared to do anything much unless he told his Secretary about it first, and found out what he had to do in return for being allowed to do it. So he knew that he had to consult her on the subjeck of Dorothy, and he decided to grit his teeth, and get the intraduction over as soon as possible.

Well, it seems that this Secretary disaproved of Dorothy from the start. And after dinner, she and the Deputy Sherif went into the front parlor, and closed the folding doors, and her disaproval finally became so loud that the Deputy Sherif had to take her out for a spin. So Dorothy tried to drownd her feelings in a magazine, but even the Baptist Beacon could not keep the tears from coming.

But from the time that the Deputy Sherif came back from his spin, he really was quite changed in his attitude toward Dorothy. I mean, he behaved as if he had some great mental strain on his mind and all his good cheer had practically vanished. And all he dared to do to Dorothy was look at her out of the corner of one eye, and keep his distants.

But he did not neglect Dorothy's education. For he had his Mother escort her to a very exclusive school, for girls only, where she could get educated up to what she was going to become. And for the first time in her life, Dorothy had the opertunity to mix with refined Christian girls of family life and learn both Truth and Honesty.

But Dorothy really did not pick up either Truth or Honesty, for the very first day in school she got into trouble, because a girl who sat in front of her asked her for the loan of a led pencil. And Dorothy had a box full, so she gave the girl half of them. Well, the girls had all been warned to be suspitious of Dorothy on account of the low envirament of a Carnaval Company that she came from. So this girl reported to the teacher that Dorothy was *giving away* led pencils. So the teacher told Dorothy to remain after school, and held an Investigation. But she found out that Dorothy did not steal them after all. So then the teacher explained to Dorothy, that the *appearance* of Evil is just as much to be avoided, and she should try to do better in the future.

And Dorothy says that while she was in that school, she was reported just like a murder trial. And the climax came one day when she was in the yard with some of the girls, and they started talking riskay, as usual. Only those girls did not tell riskay stories that had a plot and came to some cute point that was amusing, but they loved to talk riskay just for the sake of being syrupticious. Well, Dorothy soon got enough of that kind of conversation, but they seemed to be enjoying themselves so highly that Dorothy says she thought it would be a treat to tell them a story that was really funny. But, much to her surprise, it shocked the girls very much to make light of such a subjeck. So they reported Dorothy to the teacher for removing the bloom off of things that young girls ought not to mention.

So Dorothy was sent to the Principal's office and he told her that he would have to expell her, if pure girls from Christian homes got their thoughts contaminated. And he asked Dorothy if she had not learned what it meant to be a Christian, since arriving at San Diego?

So Dorothy said that, as far as she could gather, it meant everything was O.K. so long as you don't *admit* you enjoy it.

Well, then the Principal told Dorothy to wait in his office, while he went downstairs to talk her Morals over with the whole class. But as he went out of the door, he looked back and shook his finger at Dorothy and threw her a smile, and said "You little *Heathen!*" So I think he really would have liked to work up a small flirtation if he had had the virility.

Well, the Principal went down to Dorothy's class and told all the girls that Dorothy had not had the advantage of a pure home, so they must form themselves into a little Committee, and help her not to stray. And after that, Dorothy really became the center of attention, until one of the girls took a false step with a visiting football team and Dorothy lost her novelty.

But Dorothy really took no interest in her opertunities, and she finally started in to play "hookey," and wander around the City Zoo, where the perfume made her remember the Carnaval Company, and the animals took her mind off of native San Diegans.

And things finally began to get worse in the home. Because Emma started giving the Deputy Sherif darker and darker looks accompanied by low voiced remarks to herself that could be overheard. And what Emma principaly mumbled about, was the Injustice, when a girl like Dorothy lived in luxury, in a delightful bedroom, and had beautiful clothes, while Emma had not only endured the Deputy Sherif, but was expected to be an experienced chambermaid in adition. And it finaly reached a point where the Deputy Sherif would really have given Emma notice, but he could not do it, on account of the way that chambersmaids talk.

And the Deputy Sherif got practically no relief when he dropped in at his office, and had to listen to his bleach blonde

Secretary make unpleasant remarks about city constructions he had constructed, and about an Act, called the Man Act, that he had indulged in with her once, by travelling from one state to another.

But things really could not go on forever, and gradually the Deputy Sherif started in to get used to his great mental strain. And little by little he began to cast eyes at Dorothy, and be himself again. And finally one evening, he threw off all care, and decided to hear Dorothy say her prayers in a night gown.

So Dorothy had to do it, and after she got through, the Deputy Sherif decided to tuck her in, and sit on the bedside, and talk about the Purity of Girlhood. But his actions started to belie his words, and Dorothy was just getting ready to jump up and holler out the cupalow, when the Deputy Sherif suddenly began to look peculiar and fell over in a lurch, on account of some poison that Emma had put in his coffee.

Well, they sent for the doctor, and when the Deputy Sherif started in to feel better, the first thing he did was to tell everybody to keep their mouths shut, and say he was taken down with a bad case of pnewmonia. But he used his magniminity on Emma, for he did not arrest her, and he only sent her back to the Detention Home, to keep the publicity from breaking out at a trial.

But when the Deputy Sherif's Secretary found out what had occured, she decided to nurse him back to health and nothing could stop her. So she moved into the house, bag and baggage, and used so much authority that everything went under her thumb. I mean, everything except Dorothy, because she really started in to encourage Dorothy to look for trouble on the outside and it did not take Dorothy long to find it.

Chapter Six

Well, a dramatic travelling company had come to San Diego called The Frederick Morgan Players, and one Wednesday afternoon when Dorothy was playing hookey from school, as usual, she attended the matinay. Well, the production that day was called "The Tail of Two Cities" and the gentleman who portrayed the title role was Frederick Morgan himself.

And Frederick Morgan had the type of a personality that, as soon as he came out on the stage, everybody knew he was there. Because he had the habit of walking on backwards, so that the audience could not see his face. And as soon as he felt that they could hardly stand the suspence any longer, he would suddenly turn around quick and hold a pose. And Dorothy says when he did it, the thrill that went down her spine almost made her think that the back of her chair had been wired for electricity.

Well, Dorothy sat there like a trance, and never took her eyes off the Drama. And by the time Frederick Morgan had reached the last act, where he stood on the steps, and said that he was doing a better thing than he had ever done by getting hanged, the whole subjeck of Sex Appeal had taken on quite a new aspeck to Dorothy. And Dorothy says she decided that all of the things the Deputy Sherif had tried on her, that only made her squirm, would be a Horse of a different color with that leading man in the role.

So, after the matinay, Dorothy went out and stood in the lobby to gaze at his photograph. And, as Fate would have it, it seems that Frederick Morgan also had quite a habit of hurrying out in the lobby after the matinay to loiter around his photograph. So when he saw Dorothy admiring it to, he realized that they had something that was common and he gave her a kind word. And one thing led to another until Mr. Morgan invited Dorothy to have a coco cola in the back of a drug store, and tell him her Life. And from the moment he heard that Dorothy was raised in a Carnaval Company with quite an acrobatic Father, he had a fellow feeling, and he asked her if she would like to go back to the "profession"? And Dorothy was in such a seventh Heaven of delight, that she said "Yes" to an offer of $12 a week.

Well, Dorothy did not even have to bother to run away from home. Because the Deputy Sherif convalessed, but his spirits never came back, and he obeyed everything his bleach blonde Secretary told him to the letter. So when she told him that Dorothy's heart was set on a career, he held a conversation with Dorothy and said that, the way things had turned out, he could not do as he wished anyway, so he would not try to stop her. And Dorothy left the only refined home she ever had, to move into the kind of a rooming house that charges actors seven dollars a week. And two days after she left, Dorothy noted a head line in the "San Diego Union" which said, "Deputy Sherif Wins Secretary After Whirlwind Courtship." And that was how Dorothy threw away the opportunity of becoming a wealthy gentleman's bride, to start rehearsing the role of an extra girl in a bar room scene of a play called "On the Yukon."

Well, things went on until the following week, when they started to produce a promanent Broadway success where Frederick Morgan portrayed the role of a light hearted Irishman of the tenor type, who could not keep from kissing every girl he past. And he gave Dorothy the role of a girl that he past in the second act. Well, all week at rehearsal, Mr. Morgan did not bother to perform the "business," but the day the dress rehearsal arrived he started to put in the feeling. And when he did it, there was no doubt left in Dorothy's mind that she liked it.

And it seems that Mr. Morgan, himself, suddenly started to look at Dorothy in a new light, and the result was that both of them highly enjoyed the engagement.

But by the time they had played that second act for a few performances, they finally reached a point where something had to be done. So after the show on Wednesday night, Mr. Morgan invited Dorothy to accompany him to a lunch wagon for a hamburger sandwitch. And Dorothy seemed to note that when Mr. Morgan gave the waiter their order, he told him to *"leave out the onions!"*

Well, after they finished their sandwitches, Mr. Morgan told Dorothy that he had something to say, so she had better come up to his apartment. So Dorothy went. And when he got Dorothy up there, he started to tell her the story of his Life. And it seems that, in reality, he had a wife, but an artist cannot marry, so he had to send her back where he got her from, because an Artist must use all of his feelings to develop his temprament by. And then he told Dorothy that she would probably turn out to be an Artist herself, as soon as she got *her* temprament developed and found out about Life.

And he said that he himself would be willing to teach her about Life and give her all his ade. And he told her it was really quite a large opertunity for a girl like her, when society women with strings of pearls were after it. So after he finished his recommendation, he asked Dorothy whether she would like to go home, or take off her things and stay awhile.

So Dorothy took off her things.

Chapter Seven

Well, Dorothy says that as far as either she, or the Public or the critics could note, there was no more tempramant in her interpretations after she learned about Life than there had been before. But I think that what really was the matter with Dorothy was, that learning about Life did not turn out to be so enjoyable to her, after all. I mean, Dorothy is never at her best in a tate-a-tate. And nobody realized it more than Mr. Morgan. So they just let the matter drop.

Well, one week the company played at a town called Monterey that is famous for having exclusive hotels, full of the best people. And at one of them was a polo team from New York. And the Captain of the polo team was nobody else but Charlie Breene, of the famous wealthy Breene family.

Well, one day the polo team had gotten up for early-morning practise, and that gave them time to become even more intoxicated by evening than usual. So in the evening they went up to Monterey to attend the Frederick Morgan Players. But they paid very little attention to the plot and made rude remarks to the actors, and when the villain started to attack Mr. Morgan, Charlie Breene called out to "Sock him on the bustle!"

Well, things went from bad to worse, until finally Dorothy

made her entrants in the role of a maid who answered the telephone. And then the polo team began to sit up and take an interest in the drama. Well, their enthusiasm for Dorothy rose by leaps and bounds, and by the time she made her exit they would not even let the performance proceed. So I really believe that learning about "Life" must have developed Dorothy's Art, after all.

Well, the Polo team consulted their programs to learn who Dorothy was. So then they started a little chant, in unisen, and said "We want Dorothy! We want Dorothy! We want Dorothy!" and nothing could stop them. But they were so promanant that they could not be ejeckted, so finally Mr. Morgan had to send Dorothy out in front to sit with the polo team in order to keep them quiet so that he could act. And Dorothy was not needed on the stage any more as that was the last time the telephone had to ring in that drama.

Well, from the moment Dorothy joined the polo team, they calmed down and were all perfect gentlemen, especially Charlie Breene. Because it seems that he had fallen madly in love with Dorothy at first sight. But, even when Charlie calmed down, the liquor still rose to the surface and he kept breathing quite heavy breaths in Dorothy's direction and leaning on her support and mumbeling remarks that did not seem to connect with each other. And that always bores a girl like Dorothy. So after the performance when they envited her to accompany them to a champagne supper, she gave them the slip to go out with the property man. And Dorothy says that running out on millionaires has been her specialty ever since.

Well, the next day the polo team left for the south, but Charlie Breene did not forget the girl he had learned to care for. For he wrote her a letter, telling her to go right to New York and get into the Ziegfield Follies and he would see her there later. And in the letter was a "letter of introduction" to a New York broker who knew Mr. Ziegfield, and a check for $1000. But Dorothy paid no attention to the letter or the check, because Dorothy was so ignorant that she thought that money had to be in dollars and cents. I mean, I am just the reverse, because I always seem to know those things by instinck.

Well, one night Dorothy and the character actress of the company were packing up to go to Sacramento, when Dorothy happened to run across the letter from Charlie Breene. So she showed it to the character actress. Well it seems that this character actress had met a wealthy lumber magnet once in the hayday of her youth, so she knew what a check was, and she explained it all to Dorothy, and advised her to go to New York and do everything the gentleman said.

And she helped Dorothy to get ready, with the ade of a home dressmaker who went out by the day at Sacramento.

But when it came time to leave for New York, Dorothy decided that after all, Mr. Morgan had really done the best of his ability to improve her Art, so she bought him a gold headed cane. Because Dorothy is the kind of a girl that makes gentlemen presents. But I really try not to blame her, because I have a very broad mind, and I always use Psychology, so I understand that there are some people in the world who cannot help it if their instincks are unnatural. But I almost have to shudder when I think of poor Dorothy starting out all alone for a large size city full of cuter girls than she was, with less than $1000 in her pocket and practically the wrong ideas about everything.

Chapter Eight

Well, Dorothy had never learned how to dress and at a time when most girls ought to be wearing either pink or blue, Dorothy selected red which gave her such a vialent appearance that gentlemen knew at a glance she was not the kind of a girl that needs any ade. For red may make gentlemen look, but nothing holds their interest like pink or blue. And, instead of trying to make gentlemen acquaintences *herself* that would broaden her out, Dorothy spent most of her time on the train going to New York listening to a Pullman porter tell amusing experiences in a colored dialeck. So that when Dorothy arrived in New York she had not made a single gentleman acquaintance to give her a helping hand.

But Dorothy was full of confidents and she did not know she did not look like other girls. And the worst mistake she made, was that instead of carrying a small valeese, or a vanity case, or even a pocket book, Dorothy had all of her things in her armadillo basket.

Well, when Dorothy came out of the Grand Central Station, she got over onto 45th street and started to look for a hotel, and the first one she came to, she started to go in. But the taxi-starter out in front took one look at the armadillo basket and detained her, for he said they did not allow animals in that hotel. So Dorothy told him that it was nothing but a dead armadillo that couldn't have harmed him in its palmiest days. But he told her that they had never had an armadillo in their hotel, dead or alive, and who did she think she was, to break the ruling?

Well, Dorothy loves nothing so much as an argument, so she told him that if his hotel allowed alligater valeeses, where did they get off to discriminate against an armadillo? But Dorothy says she couldn't make him realize that he didn't have a leg to stand on, and quite a crowd began to gather, so she had to move on.

Well, the next hotel she came to was a very refined hotel for middle age ladies. And there were quite a few elderly ladies in the lobby when Dorothy went in. Well, Dorothy hung the armadillo basket on the arm of a chair, while she was awaiting the hotel clerck, and one of the elderly ladies happened to go over to the chair to take a seat. But just as she was taking it, she suddenly seemed to catch sight of the armadillo, and fainted. And after the confusion was over, the hotel clerck gave Dorothy quite a dark look and told her that all of their rooms were occupied. So then Dorothy went around the corner to try her luck on 44th street. But I really believe that she never would have found an exclusive hotel to except her, but that Fate always helps a girl like Dorothy.

Because the next hotel she arrived at, was the Algonquin, where all the famous actresses and movie stars live, and just as Dorothy arrived at the front door, it happened that Buster Keaton and his motion picture company were just coming in from some location, and they were still in quite amuseing comedy make-ups. So when Dorothy went into the lobby, the room clerk thought that she belonged to the comedy company and he gave her a room, and he never discovered his mistake until everybody else had cleaned up for dinner. But then it was to late to put Dorothy out, because possession is 10 points of the law.

Well, when Dorothy came down for dinner, she seemed to note that she was the center of regard. So she says she gave them all a large "dirty" look for being so rude as to stare at a girl merely because she is well dressed. And she walked quite hawtily into the special dining room that is reserved for nobody but famous actors and literary people and when George, the famous head waiter, saw her, he became so dazed that he showed her to a table. So Dorothy ordered lobster salad and chicken salad and fruit salad for dinner and decided that she was a Woman of the World at last.

Well, Dorothy began to get friendly with her waiter, as usual, and the first thing she told him, was that she had come to New York to go into the Follies. So the waiter told George, and when all the famous people asked George who Dorothy was, and George told them that she was a girl who thought she was going to get in the Follies, they were really quite amused. And finally Dorothy became the joke of the whole Algonquin hotel. And the Literary Round-Table of famous critics were really more amused than anyone. Because one of their most literary writers, Mr. Peter Hood himself, was trying to get a girl that he knew into the Follies, who really had something to offer. And he had learned how hard it is to get to Mr. Ziegfield with an intraduction.

Well, this girl was a beautiful tall immitation Russian Countess of the vampire type. And she had black hair and black eyes and quite a desperate kind of an anti-Bolshivic expression, with a leaning towards long anteek ear rings. And Dorothy says you had to give her credit, because she had almost solved the problem of how to look well groomed without the use of water. And wherever she went, people simply had to look at her, and ask one another who she was?

And what was even more unusual, she was also full of brains, for she could talk for hours and hours on almost any kind of subjeck. But the best thing she knew how to do, was to hold conversations with gentlemen about "Love." I mean, with one gentleman at a time. And she could really be just as talkative on the subjeck of 'Love' as the girl in the great novel called The Green Hat.

Well, of course, she was really much to dramatic to go into

the Follies, but she could not act in a dramatic drama on account of quite a heavy European dialeck. But as soon as she learned to taik more like an American, she was going to show we Americans her interperation of what famous writers like Mr. Strindberg meant. And she could hardly wait to get into the Follies, and meet wealthy people, who are fond of Art, and would finance her own company.

Well, it was no wonder that the whole Round-Table thought she was devine. And Peter Hood who made her discovery, could never seem to get over it. Because the first night he met her, he brought her to one of those literary parties where all the Algonquin writers who wrack their brains hard all day being amuseing, keep right on wracking their brains hard all night doing a thing called sharades, because they never seem to sit down and relax.

Well, in the midst of one of the amuseing sharades, one of the great writers who thought it up became excited over his success and dropped a lited candle onto some of the cute kind of paper caps that come out of bon bons. So the paper caps caught fire and everybody had to run out in a panic. But after they all got down in the street, and counted themselves over, they found out that one of them was missing. Well, they finally realized that it was the Russian Countess, and Peter Hood decided that, so long as he was her escort, he really ought to save her life. So he ran back into the burning building, and when he reached the apartment where the fire was, there sat this Countess, gazing at it in a revery, and saying in quite a distant voice, "Is not flame beautiful?"

Well, when Peter Hood heard her say a thing like that at a time like that, he knew that she was not like other beautiful girls. For she was full of Soul besides. And he stood there in a daze and looked at her. But by this time all the cute paper caps had dwindled down to cinders and the fire was out. Well, from that moment they all realized that she was a genius. So she was the girl that the whole Round-Table was raving about when Dorothy arrived at the Algonquin. And they all kept making engagements with Mr. Ziegfield to meet her, but he always seemed to be out. So it was no wonder they had to laugh at a girl like Dorothy.

Well, the first morning Dorothy called up the broker friend of Charlie Breene and told him that she had a letter of intraduction to him. Well, when his broker talked to Dorothy over the telephone, he was more than delighted, because there is nothing a broker really enjoys so much as getting a girl an intraduction to Mr. Ziegfield. So he said he would be right over to get Dorothy and take her out to luncheon at the Ritz. But when he met Dorothy in the lobby of the Algonquin, he looked at her, and looked at her, and he began to lose some of his interest. Because, by that time, Dorothy had discovered the immitation jewelry department at Bloomingdales, and her appearance was even more unusual than usual. So he ended up by taking her to an artistic tea room, where the way she was dressed would not be noticed.

But Dorothy does not know how to hold the interest of a broker. Because Dorothy always seems to want to make a broker laugh, which is fatal in itself. I mean the only time that brokers really want to laugh, is at a show, or when they are telling each other riskay stories on the stock exchange. For, when a broker meets a girl, he always wants to be more serious and give her good advice.

So the first thing this broker did, was to tell Dorothy that New York was a very, very wicked place. But instead of listening to him with reverants, Dorothy asked if he could give her some good addresses. So that brought the conversation to quite a halt. But the broker finally overlooked her errer, and got to feeling better. So then he told Dorothy that she should be very, very careful about what gentlemen she met, and to always ask him first whether she ought to or not. So Dorothy told him that the only one who had given her a tumble was the elevator boy at the Algonquin, but she said that if he had any objections to the elevator boy, she would take to using the staircase. So the broker began to feel very uncomfortable with a girl who did not have any awe. But he finally concentrated on his friendship for Charlie Breene, and said that he would try to help her.

Well, it turned out that this broker's only real connection with Mr. Ziegfield was that both he and Mr. Ziegfield used the same lawyer. So he invited Dorothy and the lawyer to dine and they went out to Arrow Head. Well this lawyer looked Dorothy over during the dinner, and then he told her that he had just recommended a bootlegger to Mr. Ziegfield whose Scotch turned out to be full of wood alcohol, so it would do no girl any good to have a letter of recommendation from him. So that all came to nothing.

Well, Dorothy finally reached the point where her money had run out. But Dorothy's poverty always seems to consist in not worrying about bills, so she went right on, as usual, spending most of her time in the lobby of the Algonquin hotel, becoming more and more of a chum to the elevater boy. And everybody who went in or out of the elevater always used to stop and say to Dorothy, "Well, Miss Shaw, when do you go to work for Mr. Ziegfield?" Until really Dorothy began to feel quite annoyed, so one morning she walked over to Mr. Ziegfield's offices at the New Amsterdam Theatre and became friendly with the office boy, and asked him if *he* could get her an intraduction to Mr. Ziegfield. Well, the office boy told Dorothy to wait while he went into Mr. Ziegfield's office. And finally Dorothy noted a crack appear in the doorway. And the crack finally disappeared but the office boy came out again and told Dorothy that she could enter. And that was how Dorothy came to meet Mr. Ziegfield.

Well, what happened to Dorothy really seems like almost a Miracle. Because Mr. Ziegfield got her to stand up in quite a good light, and he looked her over and over, and he smoked his cigar, and smoked his cigar, and then he finally wrote an order to Mr. Jean Buck to give her an engagement, and told her to report for rehearsal on Monday.

But after all, it was really not so much of a Miracle, as it was the Genius of Mr. Ziegfield. Because Mr. Ziegfield can see through all of a girl's bad points and pick out her good ones. And Dorothy says that most of the girls in the Follies would be passed up by practically every broker in New York, before Mr. Ziegfield has "glorified" them. Because when brokers are left to themselves, they always make a mistake and pick out some sofisticated girl that is quite well groomed, and then they keep on wondering what is the matter with her. Because hardly any broker seems to have enough Psychology to realize that the *real* ideal of his dreams is some small town village bell that he used to weave a romance around when he was age sixteen. But Mr. Ziegfield knows all about Psychology, so *that* is the kind *he* picks out. And Dorothy says that about all Mr. Ziegfield does to "glorify" them, is to get them to comb the hay out of their hair, and give up starch in lingeray.

And, as far as their street gowns are concerned, Dorothy says that Mr. Ziegfield would always rather have a girl get her models from Paris, Kentucky, than Paris, France. Because nobody knows better than Mr. Ziegfield, that there is much more glammer for brokers in dotted swiss than there ever is in crape-de-sheen. And the result of it is, that a crowd of Follies girls, off of the stage, looks like nothing so much as a small town Sunday school picnick.

And it really is a waste of time to get letters of intraduction to Mr. Ziegfield, because he gets over 20,000 of them every year, and Dorothy says that a composite photo of the whole 20,000 wouldn't even be blurred. Because they practically all say,

"Dear Mr. Ziegfield, this will introduce Miss ——— in whom I have no other interest except to assist a little girl who is full of ambition, and helping to support her family," So Dorothy says that when Mr. Ziegfield gets any such letter, it generally means that the little girl arrives in a Rols Royse, and that she has already been "glorified" with the ade of Mr. Bendel or Mr. Tappé, to a point where she has lost all of her own identity. And Dorothy says that Mr. Ziegfield's best girls wander in on their own, from 42nd street, just like she did.

Well, after Dorothy got her engagement, she went back to the Algonquin Hotel and in the lobby, she met Mr. Hood, the discoverer of the famous Russian Countess. So he came up to Dorothy, as usual, and said, "Well, Miss Shaw, when do you start in to rehearse for Mr. Ziegfield?" So when Dorothy said "Monday," he did not believe his ears. And so Dorothy showed him Mr. Ziegfield's note to Mr. Buck. Well, then he nearly fell dead. So the news got all around the lobby, and they all nearly fell dead. But when the Russian Countess heard about it, she *really* nearly fell dead. Because she had spent 8 weeks in Mr. Ziegfield's office with 10 letters of intraduction and had never even got past the office boy.

But Dorothy found out afterwards that whenever anybody sends Mr. Ziegfield some girl who is intelectual, he takes quite a good look at her first through the crack of a door. And, if she happens to be a vampire type in addition, they hardly ever meet personally. Because nobody knows better than Mr. Ziegfield that the vampire type of a girl never really gets anywheres. And there has never been a vampire type in the whole Follies. I mean, even the famous Dolores who was a very striking type of a beautiful tall brunette, was not a vampire type, but she was really a "Madonna."

And so it turned out that all of that Russian Countess's temprament and brains never got her anywheres. Because that type of a girl may interest literary gentlemen, but they are just the reverse with a broker. I mean, no broker ever really feels at home with any girl who wants to talk about such a riskay subjeck as Love. And girls who *talk* about "Love" are generally more famous for the way that gentlemen try to avoid them.

And the way everything turned out, only proves that Mr. Ziegfield is always right. For, after all, Dorothy has become one of the most famous girls in New York, in spite of all her faults, while that Russian Countess has turned out to be one of the ones who is an extra girl, whenever the Theatre Gild puts on some peasant drama about low life in Hungary.

Well, when Charlie Breene's broker friend learned that Dorothy was rehearsing in the Follies, he was nearly dumbfounded. But when he got over it, he began to realize that Dorothy was quite cute, after all. And Dorothy really did start in to become cuter, because it did not take Dorothy long to realize that something was wrong somewheres. So she gave all of her imitation jewelry and her red satin dress to the chambermaid, and bought herself a pink gingham model on Sixth Avenue and she finally got to look just like all the other girls in the Follies.

So then it seems that Charlie Breene's broker friend started in to send telegrams to Charlie out in California, boasting about how he got Dorothy into the Follies. So that seemed to make Charlie quite angry, because he sent him quite a sarcastick telegram which read—

"You make me sore. Give credit where credit is due. Who picked her out?

Charlie Breene."

Well Charlie started in to send Dorothy telegrams every day congratulating himself for picking her out. And it seems that he had to stay in California for the polo and he finally won the international polo match, but he telegraphed Dorothy that the proudest day of his life would be the party he was going to give when he got to New York, in honor of picking out a girl that got into the Follies.

Well, while Charlie was straining every nerve hurrying to New York, Dorothy was rehearsing in the Follies. And the first thing she started out to do, was to select herself a chum. But instead of becoming acquainted with famous girls, who went out socially like Peggy Hopkins, for instants, of course Dorothy started in to look farther.

Well, in the Follies there are practically always 18 Tiller girls who are an English ballay, which is noted for nothing but hard work. And they never go out anywheres socially, because they have to practise all of the time, just like soldiers. And the result, is, that they are just like one girl, on the stage and off of it. So when Dorothy was looking around for a girl friend, *that* was what she picked out.

I mean, Dorothy did not even pick out one Tiller girl. And I really think it was very undignified to go walking around the streets of New York with a whole English ballay, when she might just as well have been riding in the Rols Royse of some girl with a Future. But Dorothy says that one Tiller girl never goes out alone without yearning for the other 17. And the only reason Dorothy could think up for her selection, is that she had never in her life heard English girls talk Cockney. So she would listen to that English ballay for hours and hours, and never get through marvelling.

Well, one morning Charlie Breene finally arrived at New York. So he took Dorothy to luncheon and then he had to hurry to their country estate, to see his father, who was very, very low with pnewmonia. But he apologized to Dorothy, and told her he would be back at ten o'clock in the evening, to escort her to the party he was giving in her honor.

Well, after rehearsal was over, instead of going to her room, and relaxing for the party, Dorothy took a bus with her 18 Tiller girl chums, and went to Coney Island. And she was having such a delightful time riding on all the concessions that she forgot to look at the clock. And she never got back to the hotel until after 12, where Charlie Breene had waited in the lobby for two hours, and had gotten so nervous that he was almost ready to scream. And he finally had to escort Dorothy to a refined party full of brokers and cute girls in evening gowns, with large holes in her stockings from sliding down the Devils Slide, and practically a dislocated hip.

Chapter Nine

Well, Dorothy opened in the Follies, and Charlie Breene fell more madly in love than usual. So one night he took her for a long ride around Central Park in a closed taxi, and asked her what she wanted to do about it. Well, it seems that Dorothy did not want to do anything except get out of the taxi, because Dorothy is the cool type of temprament who quite frequently think that two is a crowd. But Dorothy hated to hurt Charlie's feelings, so she told him a "fib." I mean, she said that she was quite a vialent Catholic, and she could not do anything that might make some Catholic priest raise his eyebrows in the confessional.

Well, when Charlie found out that Dorothy was not only pure; but even religious, his love turned into Reverants, and his intentions became matramonial. So he went to his Mother, and held quite a long conversation on the subjeck of matrimony and the wonderful girl that had come into his life.

Well, it seems that Charlie Breene's Mother had always been quite anxious for him to be married, and settle down, and drink in his own home instead of in night clubs, where everybody saw him disgrace the old family name. But Mrs. Breene's choice and Charlie's never seemed to light on the same girl. Because Mrs.

Breene prefered a girl called Muriel Devanant, whose ancestors had moved in the same social set with theirs. And Muriel would make an ideal wife, because she did not care for the boys, and spent all of her time with girl friends. But I always think that Muriel really did have a small feeling for the boys, after all, because the girl friends she chose always seemed to resemble boys as closely as possible. Anyway, she was willing to strain a point and marry Charlie because of his money.

But the main reason Mrs. Breene wanted to have Muriel for a daughter-in-law was because she always knew how to do the right thing at the right time in Society. But Charlie explained to his Mother that doing the right thing at the right time in Society was only enjoyable if you enjoyed it. But when you did not, it was only a hollow sham, so he preferred a girl like Dorothy. Well, Mrs. Breene finally became very sweet, and told Charlie that she only wanted him to marry the girl of his choice. So she told him to bring Dorothy home, first, and give all the family the opertunity to make her acquaintance.

Because it seems that even if Mrs. Breene is very aristocratic, her ideas are quite broadminded, for being so wealthy. And she will always invite somebody to the home, as long as he *does* something, and when she gets him there, she always tries to make him feel as if he was almost as important as Society People, who do not *have* to do anything to be promanent.

And whenever Charlie fell madly in love with some new girl in the Follies, Mrs. Breene always liked to have him bring her home. And when she got her there, she would be very, very sweet, and draw her out in conversation about Literature, and Music and Art, so that Charlie could see how well she would fit into such a cultured envirament. But every time that Mrs. Breene did it, something fatal always seemed to happen. Because, after his Mother got through with a Follies girl, Charlie would always decide to listen to his second thoughts about weaving a Romance about a girl like that.

Well, Mrs. Breene was so anxious to have Dorothy meet her, that she told Charlie to bring Dorothy home to a family dinner. And, when the family got through with her, they would have all their Society friends come in after dinner, and meet Dorothy socially. And, in order to brighten things up, she would have some chamber music by a string quartet. Because Mrs. Breene said that, so long as Dorothy was in a musical show, she would be sure to love a string quartet. But, of course, Mrs. Breene did not know that there is hardly anything about a string quartet that apeals to a girl like Dorothy. But Charlie is such a sweet boy that he thought his Mother's idea was quite charming.

Well, just going into the old Breene family mansion on Fifth Avenue, ought to make a girl feel as if she was getting some-wheres. Because you have to be shown through three separate doors, and the first two of them are *iron*. But when Charlie show-ed Dorothy through them, all Dorothy could think of was that the Breene family were giving themselves three separate chances to throw her out, and she began to lose some of her self-possession.

Well, after they got past the third door, the butler started to lead them through quite a long, hollow hallway that had nothing to relieve it but some life size crockery baby elephants that only made Dorothy feel more unimpressive. But they finally reached the old family libery, and under an electric lamp, sat the father of Charlie Breene. But Dorothy says that, after all that sus-pence, Charlie's Father was not such a climax. I mean, he is the kind of a gentleman who has never done anything in his life, either one way or another. And the Breene family were always holding him up to Charlie as an example of what he could keep from doing if he would only concentrate his mind on it.

Well, Dorothy looked Mr. Breene over, and she began to feel quite a little better. And Mr. Breene told Dorothy that he was pleased to meet her, because somebody had taken him to a Follies once five years ago, and he really could not remember when he had ever had such an enjoyable evening. So Dorothy spoke up and said, "If you feel that way about it, why don't you take a long chance, and try going again?" So Mr. Breene said that that was really quite a bright idea, and he wondered why he had never thought of it.

And while he was wondering, Mrs. Breene came in. Well, Mrs. Breene was really more than sweet to Dorothy, for she made conversation just as if Dorothy were an equal. And first she asked Dorothy her opinion of quite a few rare old first editions of anteek classic books they had in their libery. And when Mrs. Breene asks for an opinion, she is always polite enough to stop, and wait for a reply. But Dorothy did not have any, and the atmosphere became quite strained. I mean, Dorothy does not know enough about etiquette to know that any time a girl feels like she has nothing to say, the best thing to do is to ask for a glass of water. And asking for a glass of water, where it was quite inconvenient to find one, would have made Dorothy feel quite important.

Well, after Mrs. Breene saw that Dorothy had become as uncomfortable as she could be in a libery, she invited her into the Art gallery, to show her a new picture she just brought by the famous Spanish artist called Zuluago. And Mrs. Breene told Dorothy to look it over carefully, and then tell her what she thought of its' "chiarusquero." Well, Dorothy had practically no thoughts on the subjeck, but she suddenly got quite a bright idea, and asked Charlie what *he* thought of it. So Charlie spoke up and said, "By Jove, I don't know what it is." Well, of course, it made Mrs. Breene look quite small that any son of hers was so uncultured. So she really had to bite her lip. But she became sweeter than ever to Dorothy and told her that she had arranged quite a little surprise for her. And the surprise was that she had invited Jefferson Breene, the famous uncle of Charlie, who is not only the head of the whole Breene family, but one of the most impressive Americans of the Age, to come and look her over at dinner.

Well, while they were waiting for Jefferson Breene to arrive and look Dorothy over, the famous debutant, Muriel Devanant came in and did it. Well, Muriel seemed to be delighted with Dorothy from the start, for she greeted her in quite a hearty tone, and shook Dorothy's hand in quite a strong grasp that Dorothy says reminded her of a homesick Elk meeting one of his kind in some foreign climb. But the way that Dorothy acted was the depths of being uncultured. For she backed away from Muriel, in defence, and began to look toward an exit. So finally even Charlie noted her disturbants, and he got Dorothy off on one side, and wanted to know if anything was the matter. And Dorothy said, "Nothing that an earthquake couldn't clear up." But Charlie did not understand what she was getting at. And he began to look at Dorothy askance.

Well, finally it seemed to be dinner time, and Mrs. Breene said they would not wait for Mr. Jefferson Breene, because when a gentleman holds the affairs of the Nation in his pocket, he is likely to be late at any moment. So Mrs. Breene led them through 5 or 6 large size salons with quite slippery floors and small Armenian rugs, and Dorothy says that the only difference between her and Eliza crossing the ice, was that Mrs. Breene had forgotten to order blood hounds.

Well, Dorothy said they finally arrived at the old oaken dining room, where the table was all laid out in her honor, to look like a funeral. And just as they were sitting down, the great Jefferson Breene himself came in. But when he made his entrants, Dorothy realized that she had already met him, at the apartment of a girl in the Follies called Gloria. Only at the apartment of Gloria he went under the nom de plume of Mr. Jones. Well, when Jefferson Breene was intraduced to Dorothy he was really quite surprised. But he did not seem to want to mention their previous acquaintence before the family. So he said "grace" instead.

Well, during dinner, Jefferson Breene gave Dorothy quite a confidential talk about the evils of modern life, and he finally brought up the subjeck of having met Dorothy at Gloria's apartment. So he explained to Dorothy that his interest in Gloria was to help a girl from doing wrong. Because he said that he had a theory that if gentlemen would give girls expensive apartments, and automobiles and jewelry as a reward to *keep* from doing wrong, instead of visa versa, the world would really be a better place. So he told Dorothy that that was what he was doing to Gloria. But Dorothy held her tongue, because she says the only reply she could think up to that old bird, couldn't be spoken out loud in a refined home.

Well, then Mrs. Breene started in to ask Dorothy questions

about the habits of girls in the Follies. Because it seems that Mrs. Breene was so broad minded, that she did not care how much she learned about Life. But Dorothy says that Mrs. Breene had the idea that Follies girls were about the same as red ants, and Dorothy did not know enough about red ants to answer her questions. Well, Dorothy tried to give Charlie a sign to think up a quick excuse to get out as soon as dinner was over. But Charlie did not understand, because it seems that he thought they were giving Dorothy a pleasant evening.

Well, dinner was no sooner over than the string quartet arrived. And then Society people began to pour in for the musical evening. And Mrs. Breene was so sweet to Dorothy that she picked out the most titled aristocrats to introduce her to, even if Dorothy did not know what to call them. But instead of taking the opertunity of making friends, Dorothy only let everybody see her misery. And the kind of an expression that Dorothy wears on her face when she is on the verge of standing more than she can bear, almost gives a person the impression that she is cross eyed. So the Society people began to leave Dorothy severly alone. And Mrs. Breene kept Charlie busy putting small gilt chairs all over the salon so that he could not join Dorothy and keep her company. And every time he looked at Dorothy across the salon, she was sitting all alone, looking quite unpopular, with a very unbecoming expression on her countenance. And I am really afraid that Charlie was beginning to wonder.

Well, finally Mrs. Breene came over to Dorothy and told her that she ought to smile, and enjoy herself and join in the conversation. But Dorothy does not know how to make an effort, and smile in Society, like the rest of us have to do. And finally the string quartet started in to play something that was called on the program a Bach Fudge, and Dorothy started to feel even worse.

But by this time, Mrs. Breene's own troubles began. Because nothing that Mrs. Breene could do would make those music lovers keep quiet. And just as soon as she got one set to hold their tongues in the hall, another set would start talking about themselves in the salon. And Mrs. Breene would have to crowd her way through all the gilt chairs, to tell them to "Hush!"

But, by that time, the music lovers in the hall would be at it again. And Mrs. Breene would try to hush them at a distants. But it was really like water rolling off of a duck's back. So then she would have to make her way back through all the gilt chairs in order to hush them again in the hallway. And she had to work like a Trojan, without really getting anywheres. And the looks of the string quartet kept getting blacker and blacker.

And finally things even got worse. Because somebody discovered that the butler was laying out champagne in the libery. And a regular Exodus started to occur in that direction, until there were only 4 people left in the salon, and they were the string quartet. So Mrs. Breene became almost frantick. And she rushed toward the libery, but by the time she got there, it it was jammed to the door with music lovers. Well, she finally worked her way through the crowd, and told them that the champagne would *not* be opened until the music was over, so they might just as well make up their minds to listen to the string quartet. So she pushed them all out and locked the door, and they finally decided to go back to the salon and be quiet. But Mrs. Breene did not know that one of the guests was locked up in the libery with the butler and all of that champagne. And, of course, the guest that was locked up, was Dorothy.

Well, it seems that the butler and Dorothy started right in to become friendly. For he was in quite a Bolshivistic state of mind himself, because, by rights it should have been his night out. And it seems that he was a German butler who loved music, so he had bought himself a ticket to Lowangrin at the opera. But, of course, he had to give it up. And he could not even hear the string quartet, because they had had to shut the libery door on account of the way the guests behaved. So he seemed to think that, in this world, it was only the wealthy who were allowed to love music. So he and Dorothy took a drink to forget their troubles.

Well, the champagne was of the very best, so they had some more, and the first thing Dorothy knew, she began to cheer up and feel better. And Dorothy says, that by the time the string quartet got through their program, she had reached a state where she could have been happy in a swamp. So she emerged from the libery and made her way back through the party, smiling to the right and left, and greeting people heartily that she had not even had an intraduction to.

Well, when she reached the salon, it seems that Dorothy decided to do a dance of some new step she had learned in the Follies. I mean, nobody had even asked her, but strange to say, instead of everybody being annoyed, they were all delighted. And they started to applaud. So then Dorothy decided to sing the comick version of a song that some of the girls had composed in the privacy of their own dressing room, that was not even meant to be sung in the Follies, much less a salon. But instead of being shocked, those music lovers were even more delighted, and they started to crowd back into the salon in such large numbers that the string quartet, that was trying its best to get out of the salon, nearly had its shello smashed.

Well, Dorothy became the Life of the party. And Charlie Breene stood by in pride and watched her with the love light in his eyes. And Mrs. Breene finally had to step in and take Dorothy by the arm, and make her stop. Because she told her guests that they must not allow the dear child to overtax herself.

Well, then Dorothy started to say "goodnight" to her Hostess, and quite a few guests still crowded around to listen, because by this time Dorothy had gained quite a little reputation as a "Bon Mot." So Mrs. Breene was really more than sweet to Dorothy, and she took her by the hand, and seemed to want to hold quite a little conversation. But Dorothy could not understand what she was saying because Mrs. Breene could not seem to help from breaking out into French. Well, Dorothy had learned quite a few Mexican words when she was in the Southern part of California, so Dorothy says she came right back at her in Mexican. But Dorothy really ought not to have talked Mexican to such a refined Social leader as Mrs. Breene, because hardly any society leaders know Mexican, and Dorothy was so ignorant that she did not know that it is the depths of low breeding to hold a conversation in Mexican, when the one you are holding it with does not understand the Mexican landguage.

Well, Dorothy says she finally told Mrs. Breene, in Mexican, to "help herself to the chili," and then she took Charlie by the hand and bowed herself out. And the last she saw of Mrs. Breene, she was standing in the midst of guests who admired Dorothy, gritting her teeth, and telling Charlie that he must bring his little friend again some time.

Well, when they got out, Charlie was in the seventh Heaven, because it was the first time that his Mother had ever aproved of any Follies girl enough to ask her to come again. And everybody was so full of enthusiasm about Dorothy, that Charlie was very, very proud. So he asked her to become his bride.

Well, Dorothy, as usual, was skeptical. Because she had gotten an idea that Mrs. Breene's enthusiasm was forced, and might break down before the alter. So she asked Charlie for time to think the proposition over. But Dorothy says that she really was intreeged by the idea of being able to return Mrs. Breene's hospitality by inviting *her* to their wedding breakfast. So, I mean, somethimes even a girl like Dorothy gets an impults that is sweet.

Chapter Ten

Well, Dorothy started to think it all over. But Charlie was really not the kind of a gentleman that appeals to a girl like she. Because he spent all of his time telling her that she was wonderful, and that he was nothing at all. And Dorothy prefers gentlemen who think that nothing is ideal except themselves, and let her know it. And if they except presents from her in adition, her admiration is complete. But Charlie took the wrong way to her heart and showered her with orchids, and delightful love notes, always writing something poetic like, "Oh, you wonderful girl,' for instants. And then Dorothy would decide that Charlie was not so bright, or why would he think that a girl like she was wonderful?

Well, about this time Mr. Ziegfield telegraphed to Portland, Oregon, for a band, called Henderson's Jazz Band, that had grown up on native soil, and become famous. So this jazz band finally arrived in New York and Mr. Buck worked them into the Follies. And in Henderson's jazz band there was a saxaphone player called Lester, who was only getting $65 a week. And, as a result, he started to borrow.

Well, I really feel that I do not have to write down what happened when Dorothy got in the habit of lending money to

Lester. Because at a time when a millionaire was clammering for her hand, she had to fall in Love with a saxaphone player. And the only good reason she could think of, was that the way he played the saxaphone was devine, for he was the one who came out in long moans at solo parts of the Blues. And I really suppose that a saxaphone does make a girl feel romantic, unless she has quite a lot of will power.

Well, Dorothy finally got to bringing her costumes down in the wings and changing them with the ade of a friendly stage hand, just so that she could look at the saxaphone player. And she never even thought of casting a smile at Charlie Breene, who paid $22 every night of his life to sit in the front row.

But practically all that Dorothy and the saxaphone player could do, was to gaze at one another through the wings, because the band went right from the Follies to play at the Momart for the remainder of the evening. And by the time they got through at the Momart they would have to go home and get some sleep so that they could get up and play at the Ritz for luncheon and tea.

Well, every day, Dorothy would let Charlie Breene take her to the Ritz for luncheon and tea. And every night she let him take her to the Momart for supper. And it really was pathetic, because Charlie thought that Dorothy was reaching a point where she could stand quite a lot of him. And he never knew that it was only so that she and a saxaphone player could gaze at one another. But Charlie is such a sweet boy that he hardly ever seems to notice what is going on, even when he is not drinking. And when he is drinking, he even notices less.

Well, finally at the performance one night, Dorothy and the saxaphone player encountered each other in the wings, and he told her that he was sick of the life of a jazz-band with no one to really care. So that gave Dorothy an opening, and one thing led to another until he invited her to marry him and spend her spare time keeping house. So Dorothy decided to ask the advice of two of her girl chums. And one of them was the Captain of the Tiller girls, and the other one was Gloria, the girl friend of Jefferson Breene.

Well, Gloria warned Dorothy that it would be fatal to marry a saxaphone player, without giving yourself an opertunity to get sick of him first. And she told Dorothy that it was very, very unwise to pass by Charlie Breene when the worst that could happen would be alimony.

But the Captain of the Tiller girls was full of Romance, like all girls seem to be who have not had an opertunity to meet many gentlemen. So she told Dorothy to marry the One of her choice.

Well, I do not even have to write down which was the girl chum that Dorothy listened to. For she excepted the saxaphone player, and they made a plan to go over to Jersey City on Sunday and get married. And Dorothy asked Charlie Breene for the loan of his car, but she failed to tell him what it was going to be used for. And she invited the Captain of the Tiller girls, and Mr. Henderson to go along and assist.

And then, for once in her life, Dorothy really began to get a presentment that she as doing the wrong thing. Because, on the way over to Jersey City, she got her first good look at Lester in the broad daylight, and Dorothy says she realized that he had found some place in New York City that could reproduce an Oregon haircut. And the nearer they got to Jersey City, the harder it was for Dorothy to figure out why she had done it. But it was to late to back out, because she could not spoil the whole afternoon for the Captain of the Tiller girls and Mr. Henderson, for they had their minds all made up to see a wedding. So Dorothy lived up to the bargain.

Well, that evening Dorothy had invited guests to come to a party. And Charlie had spent the whole day motoring to his father's country estate to get champagne. And after Dorothy had had quite a little champagne, she began to feel better about Lester. So she led him out of the bedroom, where he was trying to compose a telegram to break the news to the Portland Oregonian in less than 50 words, and she took him into the middle of the party and told everybody who he was.

Well, Charlie Breene could have been knocked down by less than a feather. And it really was pathetic, because he did not know what to do. I mean, he could not take a drink, because he had already done that for years. So he telephoned to the Racquet Club to buy him a ticket in the morning on the first ship that was going to sail to Europe. And then he said goodbye to Dorothy, and wished her happiness and told the saxaphone player that if he ever raised a hand to a hair of her head, in any way but kindness, he would have him to deal with in the name of the Law. But when Charlie staggered out of the doorway, Dorothy began to feel as if marrying Lester was really not such a large size acomplishment, after all.

Chapter Eleven

Well, Dorothy settled down with Lester and had an opertunity
to listen to his conversation. And that was when she seemed to
deteckt that he had started out in life as a street car conducter.
And he had learned to play the saxaphone by mail at a correspondents school to become the life of the party. But his brain
still retained the ideas of a street car conducter, and although he
constantly conversed, he really said so little that Dorothy would
finally have to tell him to save his breath for his saxaphone. And
then words would pass between them. And finally other objecks
got to passing between them, like heavy iron ornaments and
crockery ash trays, for instants, and Dorothy really began to
wonder if marriage was a failure? But Dorothy thought it all
over, and she finally decided to try and stand him, because,
after all, she had promised a Lutheran minister at New Jersey
that she would, whether she liked it or not.

And then Dorothy remembered that she had fallen in love
with him while he was playing the saxaphone, so she asked him
to bring home his saxaphone on Sunday and they would have a
musical afternoon, and she might fall in love with him all over
again. So, on Sunday afternoon, Dorothy got up and cooked him
quite a delicious breakfast, and tried to be more like a bride

228

than usual. And after breakfast she brought out the saxaphone. And Dorothy told Lester to play her some "blues," because "blues" always make Dorothy sentamental. But it turned out that the kind of "blues" that Lester played when he was all alone by himself, were to depressing for human ears to hear. And that was when Dorothy learned what a conducter means to a saxaphone player.

Well, Dorothy finally had to ask Lester to stop. But the quarrel they had when she did it, was quite vialent, and finally Dorothy locked herself up in the bedroom, and called up the Western Union to send a cablegram to Charlie Breene and ask him the name of some lawyer, because she had decided that Lester was incompatable. So Lester heard every word, and he nearly smashed the door down. And Dorothy came out, to deny his insinuations. And then he hit her with a small lamp. But Dorothy picked up an andiron in the shape of an anteek Continental soldier, and won the encounter. Only instead of aiming where it would not matter, of course Dorothy had to hit Lester on the jaw and practically ruin him for playing the saxaphone.

So Lester went to bed and staid there for days, while Dorothy had to support him. And once a husband gets in the habit of being supported, his usefulness is practically over.

But the day after the quarrel Dorothy received a cable from Charlie Breene giving her the name of a lawyer named Abels and saying that he would foot all the bills for a divorse.

So Dorothy went to Mr. Abels and told him her predicament. But it seems that Mr. Abels knew that Charlie was living on a small income that was all his family would allow. And he knew that the Breene family would not be so delighted to have Dorothy get a divorce. For Mr. Abels is the kind of a lawyer that wealthy aristocratic people in New York sometimes make use of when their sons get into an affair of the heart with a girl beneath them. So he called up Mrs. Breene and asked her, and Mrs. Breene agreed, and said that she would foot even larger bills if Mr. Abels would *pretend* to help Dorothy get a divorce, but in reality, keep her within the bounds of matramony at any cost.

229

So then Mr. Abels started in to practise his perfession. And he sent Charlie a cable saying "Don't come back to America. Trying all over again with Lester. Please don't cable me. It only makes trouble (Signed) Dorothy."

Well, Dorothy kept wondering why she did not hear again from Charlie. But Mr. Abels put her mind at rest by telling her that Mrs. Breene and Muriel Devanant had sailed for Europe, and Charlie had decided to stay in Paris to meet them. And to prove it, he showed Dorothy quite a cool cablegram from Charlie which said, "Please give Miss Shaw best wishes for happiness. Will wait here for Mother and Muriel. Regards. Charles Breene." And Dorothy felt quite depressed because, after all, Charlie was the only friend she had, that she could always count on, no matter what she did to him.

Well, Mr. Abels told Dorothy that she could not make any real move until Lester had done something to her that was illegal in the state of New York. For the only thing a New Yorker can do illegally to his wife is to admire some girl on the outside. And as Lester had long ceased to admire Dorothy, Mr. Abels told her to leave him alone, and it would only be a matter of time. Well Lester moved to a hotel, and all of Dorothy's girl friends spied on him, but he seemed to do nothing but lie in bed and read, for he never went back to work.

And Dorothy did not know that Mr. Abels was paying Lester quite a little money to keep his marriage vows sacred. And time went on, and went on, and still Lester did not show any signs of giving her evadents. For he only seemed to want to lie in bed with the Saturday Evening Post.

But finally Mr. Abels began to have his troubles. Because Lester began to wonder what good all that money was, when he was watched like a hawk, and was not allowed to entertain socially without a third party in the shape of a detecktive looking on. So he began to get nervous. And then he would have words with Mr. Abels and show his ingratitude, and threaten to tell. Well, Mr. Abels knew it was not really ingratitude but only the state of Lester's nerves, so he finally got an idea. And he sent for a nerve doctor he knew of, to calm Lester down. And this nerve doctor gave Lester a diagnosis, and prescribed the cokain habit. And that calmed him down. And from that moment Lester began to be quite a comfort to Mr. Abels. Because he developed into a regular homebody, and never seemed to want to go out of his room.

But one day Dorothy was coming out of the theatre after the matinay with Gloria, when they met a boy they knew called Claude, who used to be in the chorus, but who had practically ruined his whole career by a habit he developed of taking cokain. Well, Claude was always standing outside the stage entrants to ask the girls for the small loan of a dollar. And, when Dorothy saw him, she opened her pocket book as usual. But much to her surprise, Claude said he did not need it because he said he was getting all of the "stuff" that he wanted for nothing. And he was bubbeling over with news. For he said to Dorothy, "What do you think? I met your husband on Sixth Avenue, and he's developed into a *user*!"

Well, Dorothy was dumbfoundered, for cokain is quite expensive, and if Lester was using it, Dorothy asked what was he using for money? So Claude said, "Dearie, he's scaley with it, and living in ease on the fat of the land!"

Well, Dorothy naturally decided that Lester must have gone to work in the cokain perfession, but Claude said, "Don't be small minded! He's to wealthy to work and he's *giving* it away!" Well, then Dorothy made a remark about Lester that I can't even write down, and then Claude spoke up and said, "He may have been that *before*, dearie but *now* he's *all charm*!" For it seems that Claude thought Lester had become more artistic.

Well, after Claude went on his way, Gloria spoke up and told Dorothy that the cokain habit always seems to take away all a gentleman's interest in girls and that she would probably never get the evadents. And then Dorothy began to wonder. So then she and Gloria started in to put 2 and 2 together and came to a conclusion that Mr. Abels was back of everything and was not really Dorothy's friend at heart.

Well, Dorothy thought it would be quite a good idea to buy a revolver on Sixth Avenue and shoot him. But Gloria had an idea that was better. Because she had practically made up her mind to get Jefferson Breene to give her a trip to Paris for a vacation. So she invited Dorothy to go along, and get a Paris divorce, and enjoy her revenge by thinking of the idea that the Breene family money was footing the bills.

Chapter Twelve

Well, when Mr. Abels found out that Dorothy and Gloria were on a ship for Paris, he cabled Mrs. Breene.

So, when Mrs. Breene heard the news, she held a beautiful talk with Charlie in the Ritz bar, and told him that so long as Dorothy was settled down happily in New York with her own husband, why did he not try a trip around the world in the opasite direction? And some day, when he was in the wilds of some foreign nation, he would wake up, and the sun would be shining, and he would suddenly learn that he was all cured of his infatuation for Dorothy and send a cable to Muriel Devanant, who was a girl of his own station. And it would all work out for the best, just like it does in the Student Prince. So Charlie finally agreed to go around the world with a couriay, who was supposed to point out things for Charlie to look at. But he really was nothing more or less than a detecktive in disguise. Well, then Charlie's Mother felt so full of confidents that she began to get economical, and cabled Mr. Abels to take Lester off the family payrole.

Well, Gloria and Dorothy arrived in Paris, and they went right to the Ritz to ask for Charlie. But they learned that he was on a trip around the world with no forwarding adress. Well, the only thing for them to do, was to hunt up a French lawyer themselves, to get Dorothy a divorce. So they found the adress of one who advertised that he spoke the English landguage on the wall of a lady's retiring room in a cute cabaret at Monte Martre.

Well, the first thing this lawyer told them, was that a Paris Judge would have to see Dorothy's husband personally before he could grant her a degree. So Gloria and Dorothy had to use their wits, to get Lester to Paris. And the best friend they had to assist them turned out to be Claude.

For it seems that Claude was the type that admires abuse, while Lester was the type that knows how to supply it. And after Lester's salary from the Breene family seased, Claude invited Lester to move right into his room, and he really became more like a Mother. But Lester would only show Claude his contempt, and even throw brick-a-brack right and left, while Claude always tried to cover up the incidents that occurred.

So Gloria got in correspondents with Claude. And it seems that Lester was so angry at Mr. Abels for stopping his salary that he was delighted to come to Paris and agree to a divorce. So Gloria sent Claude the money for he and Lester to get over.

Well, the second thing the French lawyer told Dorothy to do, was to find an apartment to be her residents in a legal way. And he sent them to a French business partner friend of his who rented apartments.

Well, the apartment they found belonged to a famous French actress. And it was all furnished in the French period of decoration. I mean, wherever we Americans would have a chair, this French actress would have a couch. And wherever we would have a couch, she would have a large size double bed. And one of them was made out of a genuine Venetian gondola with a special satin matress and an awning, and another belonged to Madame Pompadore with four high bed posts that had an insense burner on the top of every one and a mirror on the ceiling. And Dorothy said that that apartment might get by as a legal residents with a French court of law, but to her mind it was the most illegal looking residents she had ever entered into.

Well, Claude and Lester arrived in Paris and became sunk in the demi monde as soon as they could find out where it was

234

located. And while the French lawyer was setting the Parisian wheels of Justice in motion, Gloria told Dorothy to relax, and look around her and get the benefit of her travels.

I mean, Gloria knows the world, for she goes abroad every year and spends all of her time in Paris. And Gloria even meets real French people. So she knows that the truth about them is, that they really have very, very high ideals. I mean, we Americans always get an opinion that the French love depravity, because they run such riskay places for we Americans to go to in Paris. But the French never go there themselves, and they really only run riskay dives for money, and not for love.

And millions of we Americans go to Paris every year without meeting a single French person socially. For the French are very exclusive, and they never think of allowing one of we Americans in their own homes. And *real* French people never meet anybody except each other, and never go anywheres except to one anothers homes. So Gloria told Dorothy to try and meet them, and learn about the world. But Dorothy said, "What do they know about the world, if they never go anywheres or meet anybody?"

So Gloria became quite angry, and finally Dorothy promised to try and become more "mon dame" which means a woman of the world, and even learn some of the French language. So Dorothy says the first word she learned from the French was the word "Sal," which always goes before the mention of foreign names. For instants, "Sal Americaines," "Sal Anglaises," "Sal Allemangs," "Sal Autruches," "Sal Italyens," etc.

And finally, one day, Dorothy had the oppertunity of meeting a genuine exclusive Frenchman. I mean, Dorothy started to walk from her apartment to the Crillon Hotel to meet Gloria for luncheon. And on the Champs Elysays this French gentleman, with a large beard, seemed to take a personal interest in her on the sidewalk. Well, Dorothy thought she must be mistaken, because Dorothy says anybody with that ammount of beard ought to be thinking about things he could really accomplish. For Dorothy had not learned that the French are very, very gallent, no matter how much of a beard they cultivate. Well,

Dorothy paid him little or no attention, but that did not seem to discourage him, so Dorothy stopped and told him that if he spent a whole week in a barber chair, he would still be outside her jurisdiction. But he did not understand the English landguage, so he kept right on.

Well, Dorothy saw two French policemen holding an arguement with each other on the street corner, so she went up and asked them to do something about it.

But the French gentleman had stepped into a small tin retiring room on the side of the curb stone. And Dorothy could not make them understand what she was getting at. But they were very polite and wanted to help one of we Americans in distress, so one of them took out his watch and showed her the time, and the other one pointed out the direction to the American Express. And then they went back to their arguement. Well, Dorothy could not do anything but go on, and sure enough, the French gentleman stepped out of his hiding place, brighter than ever, to follow.

Well Dorothy stopped once again, and warned him what was going to happen, because she thought the expression she used on her face would give him a hint, even if he did not know the words. But he seemed to be the kind that *likes* a girl of Spirit, so he kept right on.

Well, when Dorothy finally reached the Crillon, she took a quick step into the entrants and decided she had escaped him at last. But as she was standing in the lobby looking for Gloria she began to have the sensation of a beard hovering over her shoulder. So she turned around and, sure enough, there he was. Well, Dorothy lost all her endurants and gave him a slap. And to say that he was out-raged would put it quite mildly. But finally all of his manhood came to his assistance, and he hit Dorothy in the jaw and knocked her down.

Well, Gloria came up and got Dorothy on her feet to the retiring room in humiliation. For Gloria was very, very ashamed to think that an American girl would slap a French gentleman. I mean, it is things like *that* that give we Americans the reputation among the French of not having any manners.

Well, after that, Dorothy says she decided to leave the French people to go around with each other, while she went around the American Bar with all the other homesick Americans. And of course the one of her choice was Eddie Goldmark of the Goldmark Film Corporation, who had just lost all of his money. For it seems that he had had a great financial disappointment in his Life and the state that Dorothy was in, made her an ideal listener.

For, it seems that Eddie Goldmark had arrived at Paris over six months before, full of all the enthusiasm of an American motion picture magnet who was going to open a genuine American Motion Picture Palace at Paris with ventalation. So he had looked over all of the theatres in Paris, and finally he slected a large Parisian theatre on the Grand Boulevard. And his enthusiasm was intense. So he met the Frenchmen who owned the theatre, and bought and paid for it and everything seemed very, very bright.

But then he began to learn what happens to one of we Americans who starts out to renovate Paris. Because, in the first place, the Frenchmen who sold it to him were not alone in their legal rights to that theatre.

I mean, every time a theatre at Paris changes hands, the Frenchman that owned it the last time always sees to it that he holds on to some legal rights or other, that will give him an opertunity to get into any transaction that comes up, no matter when. And by the time a Parisian theatre has come down for centuries from the days of Napoleon, the number of Frenchmen who have managed to get their finger into it, one way or another, is really remarkable. So Frenchmen began to pour in on Mr. Goldmark from the four quarters of Paris, and everyone of them had some kind of a paper or other to sell that was legal. Well, Mr. Goldmark really began to lose some of his enthusiasm, because he had to pay Frenchman after Frenchman and they never seemed to run out.

But the time finally arrived at last when no more Frenchmen seemed to appear, so Mr. Goldmark made all of his plans to begin.

But that was when Mr. Goldmark learned that a Parisian theatre is Sacred, and you can not put in ventalation until you have gone up before a Govermental Committee of Architecks who want to know the reason why? Because, in the old historical days of Paris, Dorothy says that people who went to the theatre did not care what they smelled. And the French love to keep up all of the old traditions.

So this Goverment Committee soon let Mr. Goldmark know that we Americans can not come over to France and do a thing like that to a historical spot like Paris. And things began to look very, very dark to Mr. Goldmark.

But finally an influential Frenchman got him off in a corner and told him that everything would be all right for 50,000 franks. Well, Mr. Goldmark's resistants had become quite low, so he gave in and paid the 50,000 franks, and heaved quite a sigh to think that his troubles were over at last.

But they were not really over, because that very afternoon the French Ministery fell, and took the influential Frenchman with Mr. Goldmark's 50,000 franks, right down with it. And by the next morning, Mr. Goldmark had to face a whole new set of French Government officials.

Well by this time, Mr. Goldmark's determination to accomplish what he had set out to do, had become the strongest law of Nature. So he clentched his teeth and faced every new French Goverment that came up all summer long. And he paid and paid without a murmer. But anybody who knows the histry of France, and remembers how the French Ministry went right on changing day in and day out, can get an inkling of what it was costing Mr. Goldmark in dollars and cents.

But time went on, and the day, finally arrived when Mr. Goldmark had paid so many governmental Frenchmen that it had practically reached the saturation point. And no matter how obscure any new member of any new government seemed to be, he was sure to have been paid by Mr. Goldmark at one time or another.

So things were settled at last and one morning, bright and early, Mr. Goldmark started out to renovate his theatre, with

238

enough different kinds of legal papers to stop the mouth of almost anybody.

Well, Mr. Goldmark reached the lobby, and found his workmen awaiting him. So he gathered together a bevy of French plumbers, and led them into the theatre. For the first place that Mr. Goldmark had planned to attack, was the old historical French lavatoire.

Well, when they reached it, standing in the doorway, was an elderly French lavatoire attendent, with a determined look on her countenants, and a legal paper in her hand. And it did not take Mr. Goldmark long to discover that he was being invited, in French, to enter there over her dead body. So a hurry call was sent out for lawyers, and interperators, and the whole story came out.

Well, it seems that this elderly lady was called Mademoiselle Dupont and 25 years ago she had been madly in love with a Frenchman. But as time went on, the day finally came when the Frenchman had to listen to his family, and marry his fiancay. And besides, Mlle. Dupont had started in to show signs of age, and there was no use denying that it was high time for her to choose a new "maytiay" (French word for career.) So, in order to feel that she would never be in want, the Frenchman had bought her a 25 years lease on that lavatoire, as a going away present. And Mlle. Dupont had only worked out 15 years of that 25, so she had ten years to go and she stood on her rights.

Well, Mr. Goldmark took out his check book and fountain pen, as usual, and asked how much she wanted. But Mlle. Dupont said, with pride, that *her* maytiay was not for sale. Well, Mr. Goldmark thought that she was only using business methods, so he offered her more. But she refused. So then he offered her more, in franks, than all the tips she would receive for all of her natural life. But Mr. Goldmark had met his match at last. Because Mlle. Dupont not only *loved* her maytiay, but it was a matter of sentament, because it was all that she had to remember him by. So she refused to sell at any price.

And that was when Mr. Goldmark learned that there *are* French people at Paris who can not be bought and sold at every turn. And *they* are the real, genuine, honest French that we Americans are always hearing about, but practically never encounter. And we Americans meet millions of the other kind, and then we think that we have really met the French.

Well, when Mr. Goldmark heard the final verdick of Mlle. Dupont, his will power seemed to snap. For he thought it all over, and some way he could not bring himself to work up any enthusiasm in an American Motion Picture Palace with a prehistoric Parisian lavatoire. Because, in all of his dreams he had seen *two* of them, one for the ladies and one for the gentlemen, with ventalation, and water that really runs, like it does in America. And he could not bring himself to see it any other way. So Mlle. Dupont turned out to be the straw that broke the camel's back, and Mr. Goldmark gave it all up, and threw everything over. And he was only waiting around Paris until all his publicity in America had blown over and his magnet friends in New York had forgotten his boasts about showing the French nation what an American Motion Picture Palace can really be.

And that was how Dorothy wasted her time and opertunities in Paris listening to Mr. Goldmark, and passing remarks about the French Republic, until a French Judge finally took a look at Lester and granted her a degree. So Dorothy sailed back home, free at last, to "God's Country."

Chapter Thirteen

Well, Dorothy's husband finally became a drifter, and he and Claude drifted back to New York and began to follow the line of least resistants. And Dorothy says the least resistants they were able to find was in a nest of interior decorators on West 45th Street.

Well Lester spent all of his spare time trying to get an interview with Mr. Abels to find out why the Breene family had withdrawn their support, when he could tell so much that would be illegal evadents against them. Well Mr. Abels was much to promanent to waste his time with anyone like Lester, but Lester and his boy friends were talking so much against the Breene family in public places, that he finally made an appointment to let Lester come to his office and hear him out.

Well, Claude begged and begged to be allowed to accompany Lester, because after all Mr. Abels was very, very full of power and Claude was an inveterant lion hunter at heart.

So, Lester gave in at last and let Claude go along. And when they went into Mr. Abel's polished suite of mahogany offices, Claude's manners were full of reverants. For Claude believed that using the gentle tacktics would get them farther in the long run. So, as soon as they were shown to a seat, Claude spoke up and said,

"Mr. Abels, we're thrilled to be here! Lester and I often sit at home in the long evenings and read one of your famous speeches just to improve our minds."

So then Lester spoke up in quite a harsh tone and said, "You poor sap, when did we ever sit at home and read *anything*?"

Well Claude was visibly upset, and said, "Now don't be low! What kind of swine is Mr. Abels going to think we are?"

Well, then they started to give and take, and it really developed into quite a little quarrel. But Mr. Abels soon got enough of that kind of conversation, so he spoke up and told Lester to "get down to brass tacks."

But then Claude spoke up again, and said, "Justice to all is what we are after."

So then Lester said, *"Will you shut up?"* For it turned out that what *Lester* was after was $10,000, or he would tell everything to the lower type of Pictorial news sheets.

Well, Mr. Abels asked for time to consult his clients. And when he consulted the Breene family, they really went into a panick. For they had been representative Americans from the days of the Revolution, and nothing they had ever done, had ever leaked out before.

But Mr. Abels finally told them that he could keep the old Breene family name from being smirched, if they would just give him a blank card to do what he wished no matter how much it might cost them. I mean, provided they did not mind what happened to Dorothy's husband. Well, they were really at the end of their wits, so they finally told him to go ahead.

And then Mr. Abels sent for the ade of a silent business partner of his called Jerry who was the leader of the whole Brooklyn demi monde. I mean, this Jerry had a gang of "gangsters" that pretended to be bootleggers to get by the law, but they really specialized in work of a more vialent nature, such as murder, for instants.

And about two nights later, Jerry picked up an acquaintance with Lester and Claude in a public place, and took them to attend a party on the top floor of quite a high apartment house in Brooklyn. Well, Jerry's gang was full of ex-ice men of the strong male type who had been driven from their lively hood by Frigid Air, and those ex-ice men could not seem to bear Claude, and they thought that Lester was so much better by comparison that they said they thought he ought to be the one allowed to live if there was any preferance. But Jerry said to them, "What the h——, who's giving this party?" Well, they had to admit that it was Jerry. So Jerry said, "Then we'll stick to our ettiquet, and bump off the right guy!" And before the evening was over Lester got quite a lot more obnoxious, so they were all more content with the arrangements.

And about five o'clock in the morning when everybody was in the heighths of good spirits, Jerry went into a little alcove to look out the window. And then he called to Lester and said, "Come on in here, Pal, and look at the swell sunrise!". Well, Lester went into the alcove to look, but his foot must have slipped because he fell out the window. And the verdick was suicide.

Well, the funeral of Dorothy's husband was quite a novelty in the way of a funeral. For Claude borrowed the beautiful apartment of their modern Art interior decorater friend to hold it in. And it seems that Claude had his own Philosaphy, which was really more New Thought than anything, and it was really very, very beautiful.

Well, the funeral was a stag affair and Claude gathered together quite a few acquaintances and a bevy of chorus boys for the vocal numbers. And Claude had searched high and low for a very, very beautiful vase of the Grecian period, to put the ashes in, with Greek silouettes of dancers doing an anteek dance in the nude all around it. And, it seems that they were going to put the ashes in it with a beautiful ceremony Claude had thought up, that would be full of rithims.

But first of all, Claude held a beautiful talk and said that, in his Philosaphy, "It" was nothing but a beautiful journey. And Claude said he knew that Lester would want them to look at it in that way, and they must hold everything just as "he" would wish it.

So they did not break down, but they all bore up, and then

Claude brought out a bottle of very very rare old wine, and said that they were all to drink, in the spirit of Sacrafice.

Well, they all drank it, and then they were all to sing, not the kind of hyms that are uncheerful, but "It's a long, long lane," which was one of "his" favorites.

Well, they all sang harmony and then they were all to drink one more glass of Sacrafishal wine. But there was not enough Sacrafishal wine to go around, so they put it in a bowl and added some gin they had. And they all had another drink, in the spirit of Sacrafice.

Well, then Claude started to give them another talk about his Philosophy. But while he was giving it, an Art dancer called Osmer came in with a bottle of absente, so they decided to put that in the bowl and try it. And after they tried it, Claude wanted to go on with his talk. But by this time some of the other guests seemed to get the feeling that Claude was flaunting his Philosaphy as if he was the only guest at the whole funeral who had any. And it made them quite annoyed, so they all started in to tell *their* Philosophy. But it turned out to be quite confusing, because some of them were New Thought, and some were Occultism, while others were Oom, the Omnipotent. And they did not seem to be getting anywheres.

Well, Claude finally dissapeared for a moment, and when he came back he was dressed in the robes of a beautiful old anteek Grecian dancer with bare feet and a band around his head, to preceed with the ceremony of putting the ashes in the beautiful vase, that was worthy of such a contents. So he tried to call everybody to order, but by that time they had all gotten interested in other things, and finally Claude became quite ironical and said, "If you boys don't objeckt, we'll go on with the obsequies."

Well, it seems that they were still annoyed with Claude for trying to flaunt himself, and finally one of the guests who had already shown signs of becoming obnoxious, took a large drink, for courage, and spoke up and said, "You make me sick!"

Well, there was quite a lull at such a lack of reverants. But finally Claude found his tongue and spoke up, and said, "What do you mean—I make you sick?"

Well, then this guest took another large drink, and started in to tell what he *really* thought about the deseased, in no plain terms. Well, everybody was dumbfoundered, except Osmer. Because it seems that Osmer had been looking for just such an opening all evening. So he went over to the oppasition, and said, "You are right. He was a low thing to be despised by all!"

Well, it was quite a few moments before Claude could believe his own ears. But when he finally found his tongue, he spoke up and said, "I resent this!" So then quite a few resented it, and it really began to look like trouble.

Well, then the instigater of the whole thing spoke up, in quite a pointed way, and asked, "How about that time he hit you with a hair brush?"

So then Claude spoke up and said, "It was *not* a hair brush. It was a mirror, and it broke, worse luck!"

"And now," spoke up the instigater, "you have got to have seven years of misfortune!"

Well, Claude really had to admit that it was no gesture to make with a mirror, at a person who was superstitious in the first place.

And then Osmer broke in, and said, "Yes, and how about the time you had to lock him out, to keep from bodily harm? And he stuffed straw under the door and lit it?"

Well, at that, one of the others spoke up, and added fuel and said, "Yes, and the time he stood in Child's restaurant and called you vile names for all the world to hear?"

Well, Claude finally had to admit the contention, and one unpleasant reminisents led to another until they were all thoroughly fed up with the subjeck and they did not even want any mimentos around the apartment that would remind them of any such a person. So they started in to hunt for mimentos. But while they were skurrying here, there, and everywhere, Claude stubbed his bare toe on the can full of ashes. Well, that was really the last straw, for Claude's nerves had reached the snapping point. So he screamed "A wenche's curse on such as he!" and he grabbed the can full of ashes and threw them down the sink, and the funeral disperced.

Chapter Fourteen

Well, Charlie Breene's trip around the world turned out to be quite an education, because that was where he akwired all the knowledge he has learned about saki and mescal and vodka and ougapay. But finally the drinks of all the nations began to tell on him in a hospital at Shang High. But even in the midst of delerium treatments at China, where other patients would be seeing peculiar animals, Charlie always seemed to be seeing Dorothy. And the couriay had only bad news to cable Charlie's mother.

But finally Charlie and his couriay arrived at San Francisco at last, and Mrs. Breene went out to California to meet them, hoping against hope that Charlie was cured. I mean, she did not mind the delirium treatments so much, but what she really meant was Dorothy. Because after all, she was a Mother, with a Mother's love, and if her only son married the girl of his choice, he might get left out of the Social Register.

Well, when Mrs. Breene heard the truth from the couriay, she reached the depths of despondency, for Dorothy was back in New York, and free to marry anyone. So that night, she sat up late in her suite at the St. Francis Hotel, and got Mr. Abels in New York on the telephone, and told him to do something defanate to Dorothy before Charlie arrived at New York.

Well, Mr. Abels called in another one of his silent legal assistants who was more versed in the rougher kinds of law, and put the case into his hands. So this assistant thought that the best thing to do, would be to have someone put some kind of illegal dope in Dorothy's handbag, and have the police arrest Dorothy for being in its possession. And that would prove to Charlie Breene what kind of a girl he had picked out to be the Mother of his children. So an assistent lady detecktive put it in Dorothy's hand bag in the ladies room at the Club Dover, and it all worked out just as they had planned.

Well, the police took Dorothy to the station, where she had to mingle with common girls of the sidewalks, and the girl next to Dorothy was *colored*. Well, her name was Lulu, and she seemed to want to be quite friendly, so she said to Dorothy, "Hello Honey." So Dorothy said, "Hello," and then Lulu said, "What they git you for?"

Well, Dorothy was trying to fight back the tears, but she wanted to be polite. And she did not like to tell Lulu that she was innocent, because Lulu looked quite guilty, so Dorothy said, "Same thing as you, I guess." So Lulu spoke up and said, "Then I speck they pick you up for s'liciting." So then Lulu became quite thoughtful. And after she had thought quite a while, she said to Dorothy, "What they tryin' to do? *Stop that thing?*" I mean, Lulu seemed to think that the police had undertaken quite a large job.

Well, I have always said, in play, that some day Dorothy would end up in a jail, but when she finally did, I could hardly believe my ears. I mean, it is really quite a shock for a society matron who is a Mother, to be paged at 4 o'clock in the morning at the Club Lido and told that her best friend is in the station. So Henry and I went right over to see her. But by the time we arrived, theer was hardly a policeman in the whole station whose heart was in his work. Because Dorothy is the kind of a girl who is always popular with the police, and every other criminal in the whole station was being grossly neglected for Dorothy.

Well, they brought Dorothy into a small private office for

us to see. And the tears were streaming down her face, but at the same time she was trying to be brave, with the smiles coming through in a way that was practically irresistable to the authorities. And I will never, never forget how Dorothy looked up at me through her tears and said, "Well, Lorelei, I suppose we couldn't expect to keep out of here forever."

Well, the first thing Henry did was to send for Mr. Dudley Field Malone, who is one of the most famous lawyers on the side of the opressed. So he came down to the station and when he heard Dorothy's troubles, his blood boiled over. For he loves nothing better than prosecuting the wealthy kind of people who think that they can make up their own laws as they go along. And after he got through putting 2 and 2 together, he figured out that the Breene family had done enough to Dorothy to put them all in jail for 190 years without clemency.

So Mr. Malone went to the Breene family, and when he got through with them, they not only released Dorothy from jail, but they settled a sum of $500 a month damages on her for the rest of her natural life.

Well, the very next day, Charlie arrived home from his travels. And the meeting that took place between Charlie Breene and Dorothy was one of the most pathetic things that has ever occurred in the Colony restaurant. For while Henry and Dorothy and I were sitting there, eating delicious soup, we happened to look up and there was Charlie Breene. And it was really quite a shock to see what foreign travel and Oriental drinks, far from the girl of his choice had done to his personal appearance.

Well, he came over to the table shaking quite a lot. And he was so upset at seeing Dorothy at last, that he practically broke down. And it always makes me feel so sentamental to watch a gentleman break down, that I almost believe my eyes became moist. But all Dorothy said was.

"Hello Charlie, you look awful!" For Dorothy has never leatned how to be complimentary.

Well, Charlie sat down and we all had dinner, and when he heard the case that his family had trumpted up against Dorothy, he became quite an ungrateful son. For the very next day he called the whole Breene family together and told them quite a few plain Truths and got himself disinherited.

Well, then Charlie had to go to Dorothy and tell her that he did not have a penny in the world. And for the first time in Charlie's work career, he began to intreege her interest.

So I had quite a little talk with Charlie, and told him to go even further and ask Dorothy to lend him some money. So he borrowed five hundred dollars from Dorothy to get a new start in Life, selling automobiles, and Dorothy began to sit up, and take notice.

Well, it turned out that going to work seemed to make Charlie decide to stop drinking. And when he stopped drinking, he stopped feeling so humbel, because *then* he did not have anything to apologize for. And, on the contrary, he started in to become quite a bore, telling everybody else about the vileness of the bad habit of drinking in comparison with he, himself, who never touched it. And when Charlie began to give himself recommendations, he really gave Dorothy quite a little thrill.

But what really capped the climax was, that instead of always saying something complimentary to Dorothy, like, "Oh, you wonderful girl!" for instants, Charlie took to looking Dorothy over in his sober senses, and seeing her as she really was, and making remarks like, "Go wash your face! You've got on to much make-up!" And Dorothy fell in love.

Well, I told Dorothy that, under the circumstances, the ceremony ought to be in some Justice of the Peace's back office where the absents of the bridegroom's family could be overlooked by gossip. But, strange to say, Dorothy began to get very, very refined and full of ettiquet and wanted to have a large size social ceremony in a church. And it finally came out that she had wired for her Father to come clear from Modesto and give her away for the event. Well, I told Dorothy that she was taking a very great risk to have a Father give away a bride whose only public training in ettiquet had been jumping off of roofs at street fairs. And I began to become quite worried. But nothing could stop Dorothy and she went right on, and ordered steel engraved invitations from Cartiers and sent them out to not only everybody in the Social Register, but to all of her personal girl friends in the Follies besides.

Well, all of Dorothy's friends excepted, and so did all of the younger society set of the Social Register, but the older set all refused. I mean with one exception, and that was old lady Vandervent who always looks on the bright side. And she had not learned what kind of a girl Charlie was marrying, because she only reads the Christian Science Moniter and does not know all the evil that is going on in the world.

Well, the day before the ceremony Dorothy and I went down to the Grand Central Station to meet Dorothy's Father. And he got off of the train with four valises that it took two "red caps" apiece to even lift off the side walk, on account of the heavy pacific gravity of the liquor that was practically all they contained. And it seems he had made it with his own hands, and the reason he brought it to New York was not so much that he cared whose liquor he drank, as it was personal pride in his own acheevement. But I told Dorothy that that was the kind of an acheevement that adds very little to a large religious ceremony in a church.

But the way it turned out, sending for Mr. Shaw was really quite a happy thought. Because he had had quite a lot of experience handing girls down off of platforms. So when he gave Dorothy away, he did it with the most graceful gesture that I have ever seen inside of a church.

Well, after the ceremony, came the wedding reception at my salon. And I really must pay quite a few compliments to the way *a few* of us behaved. I mean, all of the girls from the Follies were overcome by the sanktity of the occasion. And even Mr. Shaw, who drank quite a lot, only became more and more gallent. But I cannot say so much for the Society set. I mean I tried quite hard to lead them a good example, by refusing champagne. But they started in to drink so heavily that finally Mrs. Vandervent came to me and said that she could not remain any longer without seeming to give them her personal sanction. But she apologized very much for the way her social born friends were acting, and she said that it was girls like Dorothy and I, who could be impressed by such an occasion, that would have to carry on the Fabric of Society. And then she said that she wanted nobody but that delightful Mr. Shaw to be her escort home

Well, I told Dorothy to give her father some kind of warning against all of his gallentry, so Dorothy got him off in one corner and said, "Pop, if you make a pass at old lady Vandervent on the way home, you take the first train out of New York society in the morning."

But the next day, Mrs. Vandervent's footman told my chauffeur and he told my maid that Dorothy's Father did "make a pass" at Mrs. Vandervent in the cabriolay, but she enjoyed it.

So, everything turned out for the best, after all, and the last I saw of Dorothy, Charlie was ordering her around on the train to Atlantic City in his sober state, and Dorothy was more refined than I have ever seen her before, with even a trace of dignity.

And it has turned out that old lady Vandervent and I have become almost inseprable, because we have practically the same ideals about everything. So I really believe that I shall be the next one to get into the Social Register, because the way they are having to put Society people out of it, somebody or other has got to take their place, and it will probably be me. And when I get in, I am going to try to get Dorothy in to, because we have been in almost everything else together. And if I *do* manage to get Dorothy into the Social Register, I shall really have to begin to believe that the world is quite a good place to live in, even in the case of a girl like Dorothy.

About the Author
Anita Loos, who died in 1981, was a newspaper
reporter, a Hollywood script writer on a
number of highly successful films and, for a
time, a Hollywood producer with her husband,
John Emerson.